A Thug Saved My Heart 2

D1568456

By: S.Yvonne

Please feel free to stay connected with me:

Facebook Personal Page:
https://www.facebook.com/shalaine.powell

Facebook Author Page:
https://www.facebook.com/author.syvonne/

Facebook Reading Group:
https://www.facebook.com/groups/506882726157516/?ref=share

Instagram Author Page:
https://instagram.com/authoress_s.yvonne?igshid=191pn9mnx922b

Recap

When I got the news of George having a heart attack I immediately went into panic mode. I'd been cuddled up on the couch with Cass watching Black Panther, while sipping some popcorn and drinking some wine. He drank a Heineken and munched on some cookies-n-cream Hershey bars since that was his thing. We'd been spending a lot of time together lately, but what impressed me the most was that he never pressured with sex or tried to make me feel like I owed him something. Day by day I was feeling that open wound in my heart closing.

I knew when I picked up the phone and heard my mama crying something was wrong. For whatever reason, I knew she was gonna say George before she even called his name and my heart sank to my ass thinking she was about to tell me he was dead. Lord, knows I wasn't prepared for that. That man had been here for me in every way possible so to lose him would be like losing another part of me. "I'm on my way ma! I'll be there soon." I panicked hopping up searching for the shoes I'd worn.

"What's up LeLe... what happen?" Cass asked me looking concerned.

"My father just had a heart attack and I need to get to Aventura hospital..." I told him with my voice cracking. I was so scared for him.

Cass didn't ask me anything else, he simply grabbed my keys off of the counter and then slid on his Gucci slides and his jacket since he already had his jeans on. "I'll drive you."

"You don't have to do that... this is a family issue."

"The fuck does that mean? You don't need to be driving alone in the condition you in all worried and shit so I'll take you. If you want me to bounce after I will... I'll come back and get you when you call."

I thought about what he said... it only took me a second to agree. "Those two big ass black niggas ain't going Cass." I referred to his bodyguards who were outside who never seemed to go too far. I still didn't understand why he even needed them. I liked Cass... a whole lot but I felt there was some shit with him that he was hiding and if he wasn't being truthful with me than we were gonna have a real big problem.

"Cool... they don't have to go... let's ride." He told me.

We walked out of the house together and were met with a set of headlights pulling up. A young, tall, dark skinned Barbie looking girl hopped out of royal blue and white Wraith dressed in designer and iced out. "Who is that?" I asked.

"What's good CoCo?" Cass asked her.

She looked him up and down. "Oh... you Cass today huh?" She smirked and rolled her eyes ignoring me. "Look man, the hot water heater is out and the garbage disposal fucking up."

"So... did you call Patrick? You know he handles all the maintenance for me."

"Now if he was answering, do you think I'd drive way over here?" She answered him like that was a no

5

brainer and then she finally acknowledged me holding out her hand to shake mine. "Hey... my name is CoCo... I'm Trey's sister."

"Oh Okay..." I smiled kinda relieved inside. "I'm LeLe... nice to meet you."

She nod her head and focused back on Cass... "Call him, or send somebody else. Please and thank you." She rolled her eyes like she really couldn't stand him and got back in her Wraith speeding off playing her music real loud.

Cass just stared at the lights until he couldn't see the car anymore. I could tell he wasn't pleased about her popping up. "Sorry about that... come on."

We both hopped in the truck and pulled off heading to the hospital. "You own other properties?" I asked since he never mentioned it. He only told me about the one other big ass house he had.

He didn't respond verbally. He only nodded his head and drove us to where we needed to go. He held my hand the entire way until we made it to the hospital. He pulled to the front entrance to let me out. "You sure you gon' be okay?" He asked.

"Yeah... go ahead. I'll call you. I just need to make sure my family is good." I assured him and after making sure that I was okay... he pulled off. I hoped he understood that I wasn't just being a bitch by not letting him stay. I just didn't want everyone in my business. This who situation with Cass and me was just different and deep down inside. I was still dealing with my heartbreak. Although it did get

better day-by-day; it still was a pain that never went anywhere.

I gave the security my I.D to scan to create me a badge and after the information desk told me what floor he was on; I took the elevator up there. My mama, Abbey, Kim, and Trell were all sitting in the waiting area. I ran to my mom wrapping my arms around her. "How he is mama?"

Still visibly shaken up, I could tell she was trying to be strong. "I.. I.. don't know LeLe... he told me he wasn't feeling well and I should've listened. I wouldn't leave bingo when he asked me to and by the time I got home, I hadn't even made it through the front door good and he fell out on the floor grabbing the left side of his chest. The pain on his face told me something was wrong and his pulse was weak so I called the ambulance. It wasn't until we got here that they told me he'd suffered a heart attack from some kind of blockage. He's in surgery now." She wiped her tears. "I was suppose to be there for my husband but I chose to sit in front of a damn Bingo table."

I wasn't even gonna sit here and throw rocks or pour salt on an open wound cause truth is, what she's saying is right. She should've been there. "Thank ya'll for coming." I smiled at Abbey and Kim. Nothing about our friendship was perfect but we always seemed to come together when it mattered the most. Kim was bat shit crazy to me but deep down inside she had a good heart. She just acted out cause she didn't know any better.

Abbey took a swig from her soda. "You know we had to be here girl... don't be thanking us."

"Right…" Kim agreed sitting with her legs crossed in the chair. Lately her ass always looked high. I can guarantee she probably smoked a joint on the way here.

Trell sat off in a chair all by himself scrolling through his phone. I stood up and grabbed his hand to pull him up. *"Walk with me…"*

He stood up. *"What's good sis?"*

"Umm has anybody called Leon? Why isn't he here? I was expecting him to be here. I know he has his own life going on but this shit isn't acceptable at all and I'm gonna tell him how I feel."

"Man I been calling that nigga for the last hour. Shit, he wont even pick up for me. He probably on the court somewhere hooping or making a money move. That's the only way I can see him not answering."

"Money move?" I frowned.

He sighed. *"Just mind ya business sis… you gotta let a man be a man."*

"Trell, I really hope ya'll aint out here doing no illegal shit cause ion want that shit around me and I'm really watching the company I keep. I don't care if ya'll are my brothers."

"Damn… whatever happened to being yo brothers keeper?" He shrugged.

"That's always Trell… you know what I meant so don't play with me. All I'm saying is don't do shit around

me… help me stay out of jail. I cant afford to be violated cause I'm cased up off somebody else shit."

He nod his head in agreement. "I got you sis."

We found ourselves in the elevator heading back down to the first floor to go outside and get some fresh air. As soon as we stepped off the elevator Leon was coming from the opposite direction and had already had a visitor tag stuck to his shirt. "Oh look… there goes Leon." I pointed.

We were both relieved to see him but he wasn't smiling at neither one of us. As a matter of fact he was focused on Trell with a mean mug. I'd never seen him looking the way he was looking right now. As he got closer the elevator next to us dinged and Abbey and Kim came off of that one. "What ya'll doing down here? Your mama told us to come get ya'll cause George just came out of surgery…" She paused noticing Leon… "what the fuck is wrong with him?" Abbey frowned and then it was like a light switch went off in her head as he got closer. "Oh shit… oh shit…" she tried to grab Leon. "Leon noooo!"

Too late, she didn't move quick enough before the left side of Trell's face was being met with Leon's right fist. That one hit caused a big ass fight. Trell didn't even know why they were fighting in the first place. We tried so hard to break the shit up as the nurses called for security but it was only so much our little asses could do compared to the size of them. "Stop ya'll!" I yelled. "What the fuck is going on here!"

Abbey tried to hard to get ahold of the situation that she was sweating. Security and the cops were running from both directions grabbing both my brothers in a chokehold as they spoke to each other through their eyes. They looked like they wanted to kill each other as they were being hauled off in cuffs. "Omgggg like whyyy man." Abbey shook her head placing her face in the palm of her hands.

I was out of breath. "Why what? Abbey what the fuck is going on?" My chest heaved up and down.

"Trell beat up Leon's boyfriend but Trell didn't actually know that was Leon's boyfriend." She sighed.

"Boyfriend?" I asked confused knowing damn well she had lost her mind. "Leon don't have no damn boyfriend. My brother ain't gay."

She nod her head. "He is LeLe... he's gay."

"HA!" Kim laughed like it was funny. "Where's the popcorn? This is better than Maury!"

"SHUT THE FUCK UP KIM!" We both yelled at her in unison just as my mama was getting off the elevator wondering where everyone was.

One look at us and she knew something was very wrong. "LeLe... what's going on?"

As if she needed any more problems right now... I had to figure out how to tell her Leon is gay and both her boys just got locked up. What a fucking day!

Chapter 1

Leandra 'LeLe' Wells

Nobody had time for Kim's bullshit. Talking about something was better than Maury, and asking for popcorn and shit. I could've just slapped the shit out of her. The fact that Abbey was even telling me that my damn brother had been living on the DL was even blowing me. "Do you hear me talking to you Leandra?" My mama snapped me from my thoughts. I mean, I heard her talking but she just sounded very far away. Almost like I was in the middle of the damn twilight zone or something.

"I'm just saying." Kim shrugged. "I guess your perfect little family isn't so perfect after all huh? I keep telling people. We all have got some shit with us. Not just me. I can bet my last dollar he didn't tell ya'll in fear of being judged."

"Kim…" I growled. "I swear to God you got one more fucking time and I'm going to beat your ass just like I used to do them bitches on the yard… now let up! I'm not tryna hurt my mama like that right now." I warned.

Abbey grabbed Kim by the arm and forced her away. "Let me talk to you real quick." She spoke as if she was dealing with her child she was about to chastise.

I focused back on my mama. "Ma… listen, Leon and Trell just got into okay? They had a big ass fight. Leon just swung on Trell out of nowhere. About what… I don't know, but right now, you need to focus on George.

Everything else can come after. I'm sure Leon will want to talk to you once he and Trell are released from jail."

"Jail?!" She screeched causing more attention to us that we didn't need. My brothers already embarrassed the shit out of me up in these people hospital fighting like two hoodlums on the fucking streets.

"Shhhh." I tried to tell her to lower her voice.

"Don't you fucking shush me LeLe. Those are 'my boys'." She pointed to herself. "Mine! And if something is going on with them I need to know. Fuck all these people!" She said like a mad woman. "My damn husband is laid up in this motherfucker after having a fresh open heart surgery. My damn twins just got locked up. My daughter is hiding shit from me, and you want me to shush? Absolutely not! Seems like ya'll being doing enough of that!"

I couldn't even believe this bullshit. I hadn't even done shit to her. Not one fucking thing and I was standing here getting yelled at and chewed the fuck out about some shit that wasn't even my shit. When them niggas gets out of jail, she better have this same fucking energy. It took everything in me not to disrespect my mama. I had to just take a deep breath. "Ma, nothing you say will get me to tell you what happened cause I don't know, and if I did, it's not my place to tell you. Now, Leon and Trell are grown. There's nothing you can do for them tonight. They have to be booked and processed. It's the weekend so they probably won't get out until Monday. If they get a bond, no worries. I'll pay it. You need to just take care of your husband ma. Take it from me, if something happens to him, you can never get him back. He's not replaceable." I told her thinking about Malik and how I would've given anything to save him.

I could tell she battled with herself. A mother's love wanted to make her run to the twins rescue. However, her obligation as a wife came first right now. "I'm going to tend to George right now because you're right. I'm telling you now though, ya'll got some fucking explain to do." She told me as I watched her get back on the same elevators she'd come off of to go back up. I needed to find Abbey.

As soon as I walked out the front sliding doors of the hospital, Abbey and Kim were walking back in. Kim spoke first. "I apologize LeLe, I was out of line. I don't know what the fuck is wrong with me some times but there's a time and a place for everything and this ain't it."

I accepted her apology, but I still wanted to smack the shit out of her ass. I nod my head and then focused on Abbey. "Abbey, how did you know that Trell beat up Leon's boyfriend? Were you there? How do you even know that he's really gay to begin with?" I quizzed. Something wasn't right. How the hell did she know all of this and I didn't?

"I saw Leon with Kevin a while back and I just never said anything. Kim told me to mind my business when I tried to get her advice as well…"

I cut her off and held one of my hands up. "Wait… holllll up. So you mean to tell me you were gonna tell Kim's nutty ass before you told me? Your best friend?"

Kim sucked her teeth at Abbey. "Bitch, don't put me in this. I had not a shit to do with this and didn't know shit about it."

Abbey frowned at her. "I didn't say you did… and I'm talking to LeLe, not you." She rolled her eyes. "Anyway, I just wanted Leon to speak on that on his time and when he felt like he was ready. I'm sorry if you feel as though I was hiding that from you." She apologized.

Kim shrugged. "Technically you were."

"Oh my Goddddd Kim…" Abbey did a little angry chuckle and cracked her knuckles. "On everything I love, you better leave me the fuck alone."

Instead of Kim saying anything else; she walked away and sat down looking unbothered.

"Okayyy." I finished. "And the whole beating up part. How do you even know about that?"

I could tell by the look in her eyes she was hiding something. Abbey and me had been down since the sandbox. We we're like peanut butter and jelly. Thelma and Louise. Kool-Aide and sugar for crying out loud. Her as couldn't lie to me. "LeLe listen, there's something I need to tell you. Well, something I should tell you at least."

"Abbey what is it? Just spit it out. Like why are you beating around the bush?"

She sucked her teeth. "Man, look LeLe. Trell and me have been seeing each other since a little after you went away. We were together when the whole fight went down. That's how I know about it." She paused. "There, I said it."

I felt like somebody had socked me in my damn chest. Everybody who knew me knew that my brothers were everything. Abbey should've been looking at Trell like a little brother instead of a fuck buddy. She had broken our number one code. Exes were off limits and so were family members. "Wow Abbey." I shook my head in disappointment. "Just... wow."

"LeLe, I promise it don't mean nothing." Her lips quivered and Abbey only got like this about people she really cared about. I didn't care though. She had sat up in my face knowing she was doing that sneaky shit behind my back.

"Really Abbey? All for some dick?"

"It's not even like that LeLe... I promise you it ain't."

"Well what is it like then Abbey, cause this shit is looking real crazy. How do we go from having a sisterhood to you fucking a lil nigga that's supposed to be like a brother to you? You don't even have any business looking at him in a way like that. I wonder what the fuck else everybody is hiding from me."

Abbey looked like she was torn between the two. I knew her and I knew she wasn't the one to back down. "And this is exactly why I didn't want you to know. Whatever happens after this, just know this doesn't change the kind of friend that I've been to you, and in all honesty you'd be dead wrong to let this come in between our friendship. None of this was planned... it just... happened.

I was so damn mad I was crying. Between George and his situation, finding out Leon is gay, both my brothers being locked up, and now here she was telling me she' basically been fucking and sucking on Trell's young ass. Hell naw, I wasn't fucking with this at all. "You know what

Abbey." I held up one hand and shook m head. "You can leave now. I got it from here." I hissed. "I don't even have shit to say to you right now."

"Now LeLe, you really gone act like this?" Abbey asked like she couldn't believe it.

Silence.

I didn't have shit else to say about it. I couldn't wait to see Trell's ass either.

Kim finally decided to come back and put her two cents in. "Now I know I'm not the most logical one here but in all reality it's just some dick." She shrugged. "She's not tryna marry the nigga."

Kim was on my last fucking nerve tonight. "Kim, for the last time, just shut the fuck up. Damn." I hissed and turned my back to walk away leaving them both standing there.

"LeLe, you really gone act like this?" Abbey's words fell on deaf ears cause I didn't have shit else to say. I decided to go check on my mama and George. I had not shit else to say to nobody for now. If it wasn't for me being on papers I would've took off on Abbey just for the disrespect. Kim's nutty ass too.

As I prepared to head inside of George's room, my mama was coming out. "You don't have to cry." She told me. "He's gonna be okay. He's resting now so they want us to let him rest. Maybe you should go on home and come back tomorrow when he's awake. He's still heavily sedated right now."

If only she knew, these tears weren't for George right now. These were tears of disappointment. Abbey was my best friend in the whole world and my loyalty would always be to my brother over here. If they were to ever take it further and it didn't work, it would complicate our friendship. I didn't want to ever be put in a position to be in the middle of any bullshit my brother may have been doing and then have to come back giving reports to Abbey. I could see it now. Trell gets a side bitch, I know about it and don't say shit than I'm the fucked up friend. Abbey decides she wants to be on some bullshit, guess what? I'm in the middle. This was the one thing we were never supposed to do to each other and she does it. Not only that, she hid it from me. Seems like everybody had some damn secrets.

I gave my mama a hug. "As long as he's okay. I'll come back tomorrow though. Are you going to be okay?" I asked her looking into her flushed face. I knew this gave her the scare she needed and if she didn't treat George better or pay him more attention than Bingo after this; then she just simply didn't deserve him and that's just that.

"I'm gonna be okay. I'm about to run home and shower and come back to stay with him overnight." She placed her hand on my shoulder. "You sure you okay Leandra? I'm ya mama. I know something else is bothering you."

"I'm okay." I lied. "You take care of George and I'mma see what's up with Leon and Trell. Don't even worry about them."

She sighed, and I know she wanted to say something else. She wanted me to tell her more, but I simply couldn't do that. Maybe we just needed to have a family meeting. I'm not gonna lie, this shit with Leon definitely blindsided me because there was never an indication. All this time I thought he had been hiding an ugly ass girlfriend when in reality he'd been getting his ass played in or vice versa. Just the thought of it was, wow. No matter what though. I loved my brother and I wish he had told me about this. This wasn't the way to find out.

Chapter 2

Leandra 'LeLe' Wells

When I made it back downstairs I sat outside on the bench and called Cass. Abbey and Kim were long gone and I was glad. Right about now. Fuck them. I had enough of my own shit going on to sit here and keep dealing with disloyal ass people.

I pulled out my phone to call Cass. No answer. I called three more times and still no answer. I felt that maybe he went to sleep or something, but he had my damn truck and I needed to get home. He talked so bad about Ubers that I no longer trusted that shit to call me a service. I wasn't trying to be the next human trafficking victim. These motherfuckers were truly losing their minds.

Since I wasn't talking to Kim or Abbey's ass, I wasn't calling them either and my brothers were definitely out of the question since both their silly asses were being booked right now. Just as I sat here thinking about who I could call my phone rang and I frowned. What the hell?

"Hello?" I answered.

"Yo, hit my line when you ready. I gotta come grab you." Trey's voice boomed through the line bringing an calmness to my ears.

"Umm okay, but where's Cass? I'm ready now." I told him.

"Okay cool… I'm on my way." He hung up.

Trey had my ass confused, all the damn time. I waited about twenty minutes and right when I was getting ready to call back he pulled up to the main entrance of the hospital and even with his tinted windows rolled up, I could hear him blasting the sounds of DJ Mustard and Roddy Ricch 'Ballin':

I put the new Forgi's on the G
I trap until the bloody bottoms is underneath
Cause all my niggas got it out the streets
I keep a hunnid racks inside my jeans

I remember hittin' the mall with the whole team
Now a nigga can't answer calls cause I'm ballin'
I was wakin' up gettin' racks in the mornin'
I was broke now I'm rich, these niggas salty

From the inside of the truck, he leaned over and opened the door for me. The cold crisp AC along with his Creed cologne hit my nostrils smelling so good. Trey wore a grey hoodie with the matching joggers. He didn't wear a big chain or none of that shit. He only wore his Rolex watch. I was so used to niggas with money being flashy, but Trey never did too much. Usually when niggas had money they wanted people to know, not Trey though. Per usual he had a serious unit on his face, always so serious. The music was so loud. I tried to reach over and turn it down. He gently slapped my hand away and turned it down himself. "What I tell you about touching a man's radio?" He shook his head. The lights from the streets bounced off of his waves since he also had the sunroof open. Looked like he had a fresh crisp tape as well.

"Whatever Trey, anybody ever tell you that you're rude as hell? Where's Cass?" I asked immediately folding my arms across my chest. "I don't appreciate him leaving me hanging and then sending you instead. What was so important that he couldn't even come?"

Trey didn't look at me. He focused on the road. "I don't know. It aint my business. I'm only doing what I was told to do. I'mma collect my bread and go about my business."

"Wow, that's it?" I asked.

"What you want me to say shorty? It aint my concern what the next man is doing. I'm my own man. This the second time I had to tell you that. I'm not about to gossip about this nigga or speak his business. To be honest, I don't really give a fuck what he's doing. Money was involved so I did this solid and that's it."

I shook my head and rest my head on the headrest. It wasn't worth saying anything else to Trey about it cause he wasn't gonna say anything about Cass or what he may have been doing. "I need my truck." I told him.

"Get it when you see him ma. I'm not going all around town to hunt this man down for a truck. It's yo fault anyway."

"How?"

"You don't ever pose to let a nigga drop you off. It's yo shit, keep it. Therefore you wont have splinters in yo ass waiting on no nigga."

"Whatever." I mumbled.

"I'm just tryna give you some free game. Take it how you want." Was all he said. I knew that was going to happen cause that's all I could ever get out of him was just a few sentences. Other than that he did his own thing.

I heard what he said but I wasn't down with him making me feel dumb. "He brought the damn truck. Was I suppose to say no?"

He shrugged. "I can't tell you what to say, but every time something like this comes up, are you going to say 'he brought the truck?'…" He asked me mimicking my voice.

"Un Un." I frowned. "I do not sound like that."

"Yeah, aiight." He turned the music back up. I immediately turned it back down. "What I tell you about that?" He shook his head stopping at a red light.

"Why don't you ever look at me when I'm talking to you?"

Trey turned his head to look at me, again, with a serious demeanor. "Why women do that dumb ass look me in the eye type of shit? I mean, a nigga can look you in the eye and still tell you whatever it is you wanna hear just to get you to shut up."

The fullness of his lips and those thick eyebrows and lashes got me, every single time. "Are you just trying to get me to shut up?" I asked.

"No, at this moment I'm not. You wanted me to look at you. I'm looking, what's up?"

"You just seem so… serious all the time. You don't smoke, you don't drink, you don't spend money being flashy, and you don't have a girl, no kids. I'm just trying to figure this out."

"You really don't know if all of the above is accurate. You assume these things cause you never seen these things around me. Never heard me talk about it. You don't know if I have a girl. You don't know if I have kids. You don't know where I live. You don't know if I smoke or drink. You don't know how much money I really have cause you haven't physically seen it." He used his pointer finger and tapped the side of his temple. "I'm a smart man."

The light turned green and he pulled off. He was absolutely right. I judged all of that based off what I'd seen and could be dead wrong. "Wow... you're right."

"Everything ain't always what it seems. Remember that." He told me. When I looked up again. We were in front of Cass's house. Trey hopped out and walked to the front porch searching for something. When he found what he was looking for, he opened the door and pulled out his gun from the small of his back before going inside the house. He came back out a few minutes later. "It's clear." He held my door open for me. "You can go in."

I furrowed my brows. "Who told you to bring me here?"

"This was my order so I'm following it. I was told to drop you here. Isn't this where you were before you went to the hospital?"

"That didn't mean I wanted to come back tonight. Nigga, I don't live here."

Trey swiped his hand down his face and blew a deep breath. "Well, you gotta stay here cause I got shit to do. I'm not going back to the hood tonight."

If he didn't wanna take me, I wasn't going to force him so I grabbed my purse and got out. "Thank you."

"Ain't no problem shorty. Lock up." He told me waiting until I was inside of Cass's house before pulling off. Even being inside of his house, Trey seemed to be on my mind. The less I knew, the more I wanted to know.

I called Cass again a few more times and he still didn't answer me. I didn't have time for this shit. I had to work in the morning and I really did want to go home. I didn't want to go upstairs so I kicked my shoes off and grabbed a throw blanket from his hall closet. Turning on the huge 75-inch flat screen TV in front of me while I scrolled Netflix looking for anything to watch. When I found 'Queen Of The South' I left it there.

I was getting ready to doze off when my phone started ringing. I swore it better had been Cass, but it wasn't. It read 'Scam Likely'. Usually I didn't answer these kind of calls but due to the circumstances with my brothers, I did. It was a free call from Trell. "We can't see a judge until we go to magistrate court on Monday morning and most likely they'll give us a bond."

I didn't want to try to talk to him about what happened while he was in that place. There was a time and place for everything and now wasn't the time. "I'll be there. I'll take care of the bond."

"Yeah, I'll give you the bread back as soon as I jump." He told me sounding hurt. I knew he was. He and Leon had never fought each other. Ever.

"Okay. Just stick it out a few more days. I love you." I told him before hanging up.

~~~~~~~~

The next morning I was waking up to the sun being out and the sounds of Cass walking through the door. In his hand, he had a dozen of red roses and some carryout containers with breakfast food in it. He looked well refreshed as well. He didn't look like he missed any damn sleep. Hell, he didn't even have on the same shit he had on when he dropped me off. I immediately put my shoes on and grilled him. "Naw Cass... not cool at all. After the night I had last night you don't even show up for me, don't answer my calls and then leave me stranded here with no car."

Cass looked good as hell. Even though I was pissed the fuck off with him. He wore a simple black suit but for whatever reason his collar shirt nor his jacket were buttoned down exposing his ripped 8 pack. He placed the food and the keys on the counter and walked over to me with the roses. "You mad at me?" He hugged me lifting me off the ground while nuzzling his face into the side of my neck. I made a mental note that he smelled like fresh soap as well.

"Put me down." I sassed. "Listen, I'm not your girl so if you out doing your little one two or whatever that's cool with me. You have no reason to lie to me at all. However, you have to be respectful about what you're doing. How the hell do you leave me hanging? Send Trey to get me, and then leave me at 'your house' alone, literally all night and then you walk through the door smelling like fresh soap like you've been fucking all night and had to wash it off before you came here?"

Cass just stared at me and let me vent. "You done ma?"

I sucked my teeth. "Cass, you know what, I don't have time for this. I need to get home and shower to get ready for work. You know, cook the food for your restaurant to make sure all those flyy ass bitches keeps coming back." I attempt to walk past him, which prompted him to gently grab my arm. Leaning down, he kissed my lips.

"You know you real cute when you're mad?" He told me.

I sucked my teeth again. "Un Un I gotta to go."

"Alright Alright…" He decided to stop fucking with me. "I know the shit looks crazy but I got caught up in work last night. I had Trey come and get you cause I knew I'd probably be tied up and I had every intention on coming here. I told you I have another house as well. By the time he got you and you were blowing me up I had done already fell asleep."

I didn't know who he thought he was fooling, but if that's the story he thought was going to make me feel like his actions were acceptable he had me all wrong. It was going to take more than some damn flowers to fix my attitude right now. "Okay." I replied while grabbing the keys off of the counter. "I'll see you at work." I left him standing there with his damn roses and his breakfast.

I sat in the truck a few minutes before pulling off. Cass didn't come after me cause he was too busy studying me. I knew what he was doing. He was trying to learn me. May have been a little gullible, but definitely not dumb. I made it home just in time to shower, grab my recipe book, and head to work. As soon as I walked in, the girl Ayana who worked the cash register was wiping down tables and making preparations to open in a few hours. When she spotted me, she handed me a piece of paper. "Here LeLe, some dude came by here looking for you. He wrote his number down on a piece of paper. His name is Kevin and he's real pretty too."

I frowned looking down at the number and the name scribbled. "I know damn well Leon's lover don't wanna talk to me." I mumbled. "Un Un this is just too much." I put the piece of paper in my apron and made my way to the back to get my day started. As soon as I put on a big pot of collard greens, Trey called me. "Um Hello?" I answered unsure of what he may have wanted.

"You okay? Made it to work aiight?"

"Everything is everything." I assured him.

"Aiight… cool. Enjoy ya day shorty."

"But Trey wait…"

It was too damn late cause he'd already hung up on me. I was going to get down to some facts about his mysterious ass as soon as I dealt with my own personal shit.

Chapter 3

Majestic Jones

"Come here." I told Kim as she used her hands aggressively removing my shirt. She had been on some other shit lately, and I know fucking was one thing and I was cool with that, but now she was just treating a nigga like a straight up slut bitch. All she wanted to do was jump on the dick. Get hers and then get the fuck on. The past few days it seemed like she wasn't even here mentally. Like her body was here, but her mind was always drifting. "Slow down." I told her gently grabbing her by the wrist. She looked up at me and smacked her lips with an attitude.

"Listen, either you gonna give me some dick or you not cause if not you can go."

"First of all ion know who the fuck you talking to and second, you not finna just keep jumping on a nigga like a wild fucking animal. Be a fucking lady Kim."

Ignoring my words, she reached up and placed a hard kiss on my lips. Then another one following that one up. A nigga just shook his head and decided to play her game. "You wanna be fucked like a slut? Cool."

I pushed her down on the bed and then flipped her over watching spread her ass cheeks and put a deep arch in her back since she was already naked. I couldn't even ignore the throbbing in my hard dick looking at such a beautiful ass sight. Kim was bat shit crazy in my book, but it was no denying how beautiful of a woman she truly is. Not to mention the bitch is built like a stallion. I unzipped my jeans and pulled my dick from my boxers before plunging it into her awaiting pussy.

"Ahhhhh! Ouuuuu shit!" Kim closed her eyes and started bucking back throwing that ass in a circle. Without a conscience, I fucked Kim just like the slut she wanted to be fucked liked as my groans and sounds of skin smacking echoed through the room. Slapping her ass, I watched it jiggle and immediately form a red mark. Wasn't even no denying how good her pussy was. Then again, it was always the craziest bitches with the best pussy. "Choke me!" She demanded.

This bitch losing her fucking mind. I thought to myself taking my hand wrapping it around her neck still fucking her doggy style, while roughly grabbing her. I felt my shit about to cum trying to ignore how good it felt. Kim had my dick stupid wet. "Ouuuu I'm about to cum!" She squealed. "Choke me harder!" She demanded.

I squeezed harder in my own zone not even realizing that Kim was barely throwing it back when I felt her climaxing all over my dick, it was weak as fuck. I pulled out watching pre-cum ooze from the tip of my dick and let her go. "Yo Kim, what kinda shit you on?" She lazily dropped her body on the bed. For the first time, I noticed how red her face was and the tears coming from her eyes. "What the fuck?" I furrowed my brows and scratched my head. I stuffed my shit back in my boxers and pulled my pants up. "Kim, what the fuck really going on?" If I didn't know any better I'd say she was trying to make me kill her ass on purpose.

"I didn't have the guts to do it." She said in almost a whisper.

I grabbed my keys from the dresser shaking my head. "Do what? Man you wildin' and I keep telling yo ass you need fucking help! You wanna die? Cool but do that shit on your own time ma. A nigga ain't feelin' this shit at all."

"Just get out Majestic. I'll be fine. I'm aiight and ion need Nan motherfucker preaching to me."

A few seconds ago I was really ready to walk out this bitch, however, looking at the state she was in I couldn't even do it. What if I left and this crazy muhfucka really did try to kill herself? I'd never be able to live with myself knowing I could've stopped it. Regardless of how Kim wanted me to feel about her trifling stanking ass, I realized that I did start to develop some kind of feelings for her, and not because she was a likeable person; Lord knows she ain't. It was her demonic struggle that made me care. I knew I had demons, but Kim's shit was deathly. She couldn't even keep her eyes open long enough to fuss with me.

When she closed her eyes, I tossed the cover over her naked body and went in her bathroom to wash myself of her lingering juices off of my manhood. I had been moving nonstop so I wasn't even surprised looking at myself in the mirror and noticing how red my eyes were. Opening her medicine cabinet, I searched for some eye drops. The box was staring me in my face. Much to my surprise though, when I opened the box it wasn't what it was supposed to be. It was a tiny back of coke in it tied up. I had to make sure I was seeing what the fuck I was really seeing. I mean, the drug itself wasn't a shocker to me. What the fuck was it doing in Kim's medicine cabinet hidden just like some ole crack head shit?

I took the bag and walked back out to Kim's room snatching the covers off of her. She didn't even open her eyes, she only shivered and remained sleep. "Yo Kim!" I shook her body. "Kim! Wake yo ass up!" I forcefully snatched her up forcing her to look at me. Her eyes barely opened.

"What Majestic? Can you leave me the fuck alone? I'm not feeling well."

I dangled the dope in her face. "What the fuck is this Kim? You snorting and shit? You a fucking coke head now?"

She sighed and dropped her eyes. I knew right then it was her shit. I let her go allowing her to fall back on the bed where she grabbed the covers and pulled them back over her body. "Yo, this shit is crazy man. You a real fucking coke head out here. What the fuck is wrong with you?!" I dumped the contents of the bag in the toilet and walked back in the room. Wasn't even no need in me to keep fussing cause she went right back to sleep. Her ass was probably high as a kite right now. Her behavior made perfect sense. This shit was getting too deep. Me even fucking with Kim could be a great liability but I couldn't help it. I had to try to help this girl if I could. If she would just let me.

Fuck our current situation. We were still childhood friends and I hated to see her go out like that. I stayed as long as I could before it was time for me to head out. I wasn't getting paid to babysit Kim all day. I had to go make money selling the same shit that she'd become a victim to. This circle of life was fucked up sometimes. I made sure I locked her door before I left and even when I made it out to my whip I sat there and broke down some weed in my lap before rolling me a joint and taking a few puffs to get my mind right.

I didn't know who else to call. Calling LeLe was out of the question. Besides, I didn't have the bitch's new number anyway. I wasn't about to pass no messages through Poochie's ass either cause I no longer trusted this nigga. Malik was like a little brother to him but now it seemed like he was falling for LeLe's ass so I decided to just sit back and watch it play out.

I called Abbey instead. "Yo…"

"What? I had a rough couple of days and you're the last person I expected to be calling me, so what do you want?" She immediately snapped. I don't know if it was just me or if all these bitches were losing their minds.

"Look you need to come check on ya girl Kim. She's on some other shit."

She sucked her teeth. "What did she do now? Cause I'm low key not fucking with her simple ass."

"Yeah, well, ya friend in there all coked up and she needs somebody with some sense here when she wakes up cause I'm leaving."

"What?! You a real piece of shit Majestic. You just gone fuck and leave knowing the girl is fucked up."

"First of all, you don't know shit and I aint explaining. If you care then get here cause I'm out." I hung up the phone. I wasn't arguing with Nan female today, fuck that shit.

33

Chapter 4

Abbey Daniels

I wasn't even going to go to Kim's house after Majestic called but after thinking about it, I'd feel bad if something happened to her and I didn't go. After a short battle with myself, I grabbed my keys and drove over to her place. I hadn't spoken to her in a few days. Matter of fact, haven't spoke to her ass since we left the hospital cause she was on some straight bullshit and that mouth had no filter on it. I had to smoke me a joint first before I went to her place so I sat in my car and pulled out the half that I had inside of my purse and turned on the music positioning the air directly in my face while opening the sunroof. 99-Jamz was playing 'Act Up' by the City Girls so I turned that up a little and vibe out until I was finished smoking.

I pulled out my bottle of Dior perfume from my purse and sprayed a little before popping a mint in my mouth and pulling off. When I got to Kim's apartment I had to park in the building behind hers and then take the walk to her door. I knew she kept a spare key inside of the porch light, so I grabbed it making sure nobody was watching before I walked inside. There was a figure on the couch that scared the shit out of me. I grabbed my chest. "Oh shit Kim! You scared the fuck out of me." I marched to the window and pulled her blinds back to let some light inside. "Why you sitting here in the dark? And what the fuck is going on with you?" I fold both my arms across my chest and waited for an answer.

She was sitting there with a blanket on her sipping on something out of her coffee mug. To the naked eye she looked normal. It's not like she looked like shit or nothing like that. "What are you even doing in my house?" She sassed.

"Majestic called me."

She chuckled. "Everybody wants to be in my business but wont worry about their own shit."

See, this the shit that always made me want to slap the taste out of her mouth. "I'm just gone ignore your slick ass mouth. Whether we beefing or not this is what 'real' friends do. Speaking to you or not I'm not going to sit here and let you just sulk into a depression like this." Before I knew it, I was pacing the floor.

The only thing that stopped me was the ringing from my phone. I looked at the call from Trell and ignored it. He had been out of jail for 24 hours and called me as soon as he got out. I hadn't accepted not one damn call. Because of him, I lost my best friend. "Gone and pick up the man calls Abbey. Shit, the cat is out the bag. Or let me guess. You're blaming him cause you chose to open your legs." Kim shrugged. "It aint his fault. You need to own your shit too. If LeLe don't like it than oh fucking well. Make her like it."

I wasn't sure how she even knew that was Trell calling me, but I refused to even address this with Kim right now. No matter how crazy she was though, sometimes she just kept that shit too real and a lot of people couldn't deal with her because of that. Since I was off for the nest few days I had a bright idea. "Pack up for a few days. Let's make that trip to see Karter." I suggested.

Kim immediately stood up allowing the blanket that was around her to fall to a puddle around her bare feet.

"Finally." She rolled her eyes. "You speaking some shit I actually wanna hear."

Within a few seconds she disappeared in the back room. I pulled my phone out and read a text from Trell.

From Trell: Don't make me pull up.

To Trell: Stop calling me! Just fuck it aiight.

I had a full-blown attitude. I didn't like this shit of a feeling. I waited for Kim to come back out and when she did, we hopped in my car so I could go put me together a bag as well. We decided we didn't want to call Karter cause we wanted to surprise her anyway and since she didn't work right now, we knew she wasn't doing shit besides sitting in the house waiting to have that baby. I made sure I gassed up and then I stopped to grab some burgers for Kim and me to eat before hopping on the road. I purposely turned the music all the way up just in case Kim started with her shit. I thought the perfect song for how I was feeling would be Letoya Luckett 'Torn'

I snapped my fingers and vibe to the music:

What hurts the most is when we started out
It was cool; it was everything that loves about
But something happened cause I'm feeling so burned out

You got me just torn in between the two
Cause I really wanna be with you
But something is telling me that I should leave you alone
You alone (leave you alone, leave you alone)

It didn't take us no time to get to Orlando. I mean, we stopped once for more gas and to pee but that was it and

I was so glad Kim behaved and actually had decent conversation with me. When we pulled up in Karter's driveway there was only one car parked in the front. A brand new black on black Cadillac Escalade truck. We didn't even bother to get our bags, we walked to the door to ring the bell but after a few minutes there still wasn't an answer. We prepared to walk away when we heard the door unlocking. Staring at a middle-aged black woman, she had on an apron and the house smelled like cleaning supplies. "Can I help you?" She asked.

"Um yes. I'm looking for my sister. Karter." Kim didn't even attempt to give the lady an friendly smile or anything.

I intervened extending my hand to hers and smile. "Hi, we're her family and we were trying to surprise her."

Seemed like she took to me a little better. "Oh… nice meeting you. She's speaks of her family a lot, but she's not here. She didn't tell you all she had the baby last night? She probably wanted to surprise you."

"Um yes, that's probably what happened. Can we have the hospital name please?" I asked her.

Kim threw her shades on her face and walked back to the car while I got the information. "I'm not even surprised." She mumbled.

"Why you so rude?" I asked Kim when I got back in the car. She held one hand up to me to stop me from talking. She was on the phone with somebody or waiting for them to pick up.

"Hey there mother. Yeah, it's me Kim. The devil's daughter or whatever you want to call me. I was just wondering if you knew that Karter had the baby last night." She said while I listened from Kim's end. "Oh is that right? Well how far are you from the hospital? I'm not even surprised that you didn't think to call me." I ear hustled a little more until Kim hung up the phone.

I backed out of the driveway to head to the hospital. "What's the real deal with you and yo mama girl? Like seriously." I asked her.

"Nothing that I want to talk about. The bitch don't like me. Simple." She shrugged. "Anyway, she just reached Orlando and she's headed to the hospital. She claims that Karter's fiancé is out of town on business and her water broke last night. She wasn't scheduled to be induced until next week. I guess she didn't want to be alone so she called our mama. But whatever."

I nod my head. "Okay but why doesn't she like you?"

"Listen, I don't want to talk about it." She warned me again.

I turned the music back up. Fuck it, if she didn't want to talk to me then I wasn't going to force her but apparently whatever issues they had was really fucking with her. After dealing with traffic, we pulled up to the hospital and hopped out. Sure enough, Karter had her baby girl and was in the maternity ward recovering. I did feel a way that she didn't call, but since I'm not a mother I couldn't even try to come up with my own theories as into why. Maybe she wanted this time alone, maybe she didn't want to share her baby with the world yet. Whatever it was, I would presume to try to understand.

We stopped to the gift shop first to grab some flowers and balloons. I wanted to call LeLe and let her know Karter had the baby but at the same time, I didn't want her to hang up on me or just simply ignore my call. I knew we would get back right soon. LeLe just needed some time and I understood that. I hoped she wasn't too mad. If leaving Trell alone is what she wanted, that's what I was willing to do and that's why I'd already started the process of trying. Kim I me both lingered in our own thoughts on the elevator ride up to maternity before we found Karter's room. We knocked on the door until we heard her squeaky voice telling us to come in. As soon as she saw us she looked shocked while we wore smiles on our faces. "Omgggg you had the baby!" I squealed.

Kim took her glasses off. "Surprise sis." She rubbed both of her hands together. "Where's my niece?" We scanned the room for the baby, but the baby wasn't here.

Karter sat up in the bed wearing her pink robe. Her long natural hair was braided back in a long cornrow. "I... hi... what are you guys doing here?"

I frowned. "Um are you not happy to see us? Where's the baby? I can't believe you didn't call us."

"I just didn't want to disturb anyone until I knew everything was okay." She said still looking kinda uneasy. "The baby went to get some shots and test ran with the nurse but she'll be back."

"What did you name her?" Kim asked flopping down on the chair after she put our flowers and balloons on

40

the table. There were also other flowers and balloons beside ours.

"Her name is Barbie Bella."

"Um… okay… it's your baby." Kim gave a slight smile.

"I think it's beautiful." I told her.

"So when's Barbie coming back? And when is the fiancé coming back in town? You know ma is on the way?" Said Kim.

Karter nod her head. "Yes, I called her to be here with me cause my fiancé wont get back until this weekend."

There was an awkward silence that filled the room. None of us knew what to say. Gladly there was another knock on the door and in came a tall white woman with blonde hair and green eyes. She was beautiful but kind of butch looking. She didn't even acknowledge us at first. Her only focus was Karter. Rushing to her side, Karter froze up and so did we when she placed a heavy kiss on Karter's lips. "Omg babe I got here as soon as I could. I was worried sick about you!" She lovingly rubbed the side of Karter's face embracing her in a hug.

"Babe!" Karter squealed. "What are you doing here? You're not supposed to be here yet."

"Babe?!!!!" Kim and me blurted.

The white woman finally looked at us. "Oh, I'm sorry. How rude. I'm Emily, Karter's fiancé." She extended her hand to ours. We couldn't even say shit, just shook her hand with confused looks on our faces. She was so engulfed in Karter that she didn't even notice as she focused her attention back on her placing more kisses on Karter's face. She didn't even realize that Karter wasn't showing her the same affection.

There was another knock on the door and Karter and Kim's mother was walking in with balloons in her hands but her smile suddenly turned into a frown. "Karter! Who the hell is this white woman kissing all over you?" She demanded answers even looking at us for some clarification. Shit, we had none.

Karter dropped her face in the palm of her hands too embarrassed. I fucking knew it! I knew she was hiding something. Yeah, I wanted to know what happened to all that black power shit just like everyone else did.

"Pick your face up off the floor 'Black Queen'." Kim taunted her mother.

"Kim! Don't start!" I told her. I redirected my attention to Karter. "Um Karter, what's going on here?"

She took a deep breath and sighed. She never did like the feeling of all eyes being on her.

Chapter 5

Leon Wells

After spending a weekend in jail for fighting with Trell's muhfuckin' ass. I had so much pressure built up in me that anybody could get this work. I spent the next two days in practice and in the gym. The lawyer LeLe had for us was working on getting the case dismissed so neither one of us had to deal with this shit. I didn't have shit to say to my brother right now, but I do regret losing it like that. When Kevin called me and told me what happened I was pissed. I mean, true, Kevin initiated it in the worst case of mistaken identity but still; Trell did too fucking much. I wasn't too happy to see Kevin's face fucked up like that and with a fractured jaw. He didn't even look like himself. I had yet to make it to see him since I'd been released and talking to him on the phone was pointless cause I doubt he wanted to hear shit I had to say.

I tossed my gym bag in my trunk and pulled out the piece of paper Kevin handed me in the hospital that simply read: *You're family will never accept me. I don't want to see you again.* After the way Trell did him. I couldn't even blame him for not wanting to see me. I personally didn't even know what to say to him at this point but each day was getting harder not talking to him. I know I needed to check on George too cause I still hadn't seen him and he was still in the hospital. After making my rounds, that's what I did. I made my way to the hospital. George was alone and sleeping so I didn't want to bother the old man. I made sure I left some 'Get Well' balloons with a card so he would know I'd been here.

I didn't understand why he was alone in the first place. My mama bet not had her ass at bingo so I called her as soon as I got back in the car. "I hope you ain't at bingo." I told her.

"I'm home cooking for my husband so he doesn't have to eat anymore hospital food when he wakes up from his nap. Where are you anyway? I need you to get your ass here. I need to speak to you." She demanded. "And right now."

I might at well have got this over with. "Say less. I'll be there in fifteen minutes but if Trell is there don't even hold ya breath."

"He's not."

"Good." I hung up. I had been staying in a hotel since I got out; just because I didn't want to run into Trell. A bigger part of me just simply didn't know how to face him. My brother hated gays and here I am, having to accept the fact that it was what it was. I know if anything he was more hurt when he found out the truth. I wished this shit could've played out another way. If only Kevin had just kept his mouth shut. Instead, he dropped the ball on a nigga. "Mama!" I yelled when I opened up the door. She was still in the kitchen cooking and my stomach immediately started talking to me. Felt like I hadn't eaten in days.

"Oh boy, stop your damn yelling. I'm in here." She sat the spoon on the counter and removed her apron. "Now, you know why I called you here don't you? We need to talk."

I wiped my hand down my face and blew hard. "About what?"

"You know about what Leon. Now Trell told me the real reason you jumped on him. I need answers cause I know damn well what he told me couldn't have been true because I didn't raise you that way. So tell me."

I frowned. "Tell you what ma?"

She took her pointer finger using it to mush me right in the middle of my forehead. "Don't play games with me son. Are you gay?"

I probably could've openly spoke to her if she wasn't giving me the fucked up and most hurtful look I'd ever seen her give me. "I don't like that word."

"Fuck that son. It's either you're gay or you're not. I didn't raise you to be no damn faggot!"

I shook my head. "Look at me ma. Do I look like a fucking faggot? Do you know what a faggot is?"

"Don't you get smart with me. I know exactly what a faggot is and it ain't my damn son. Now whatever the hell is going on you need to get that shit up outta you, or else I'll beat it out of you." She wiped a single angry tear from her eye. "I mean it! And you better apologize to your damn brother. How dare you be around here fighting him over a nigga! That's some real bitch shit!"

I don't even know why she called me over here to talk, cause she wasn't giving me a chance to say not a shit. Not one fucking word. Since I was here. I needed to tell her what was on my mind. I couldn't be around them and have them acting this way. They didn't accept me for who I am, and that's the most frustrating part. "I'm getting my own apartment ma. I can't do this here no more. Not like this."

She looked like I'd knocked the wind out of her with my news. "So your little dirty trapped in the closet secret gets out and you want to run? That's not how we deal with family issues!" She said picking up the fly swatter popping the shit out of my arm. That shit stung so damn bad but I couldn't hit my mama although I wanted to fuck her ass up.

I stood up and grabbed my keys. "You know what ma. I'mma head on out."

Too bad I didn't leave sooner cause Trell came walking through the front door but as soon as he seen my face her wore a mug on his. "What's up ma." He spoke and rushed past us both to the back room like he was in a hurry. The nigga ain't acknowledge me and I didn't acknowledge him either since neither one of us didn't wanna address the elephant in the room. When he came back out to leave, my mama stopped him.

"Well ain't you gone speak to your brother?" She asked grabbing his arm.

He snatched away from her without giving too much force. "Ion got no brother." He walked out closing the door behind him.

She started to run after him but I stopped her. "Nah ma, let the nigga go. You can't fix this. Can't nobody fix this besides me and Trell. Simple as that."

"Leon, you did start it. You fought him! You're the last person he would've expected that out of. You were wrong. If anything he's more hurt behind your actions!"

I heard what she was saying but I knew better. Trell may have been hurt behind what I did. However, it was his pride over everything else knowing that his twin brother was bisexual. We're some hood niggas. It wasn't supposed to be like this. I didn't know how long it would take us to make it right but I knew something had to give. In the meantime though, I would be finding my own spot. I didn't attempt to say anything else. I just simply walked out and was surprised she let me.

I knew I said I wasn't going to go to Kevin's house, but at a time like this I just didn't know whom else I should talk to. If anybody knew what it was like coming out of the closet and shit, it had to be Kevin cause at one point he was in this same predicament as me. I didn't turn on the radio or nothing. I just drove in silence cause that was the best way to think. I was about ten minutes away from his house when I received a call from Majestic. "Yo?" I answered not really feeling like being bothered with this nigga today.

"I know you been locked up and all but a nigga ain't seen yo face but once since you got home. I come to the spot, you done been there and left already. Nigga we been doing numbers the same for the past few months so what's up?"

"Shit, ain't nothin' just tryna get my head back in the right space bro. Everything is everything though." I assured him. One thing about it; he didn't have to worry about me on the money tip on my end cause I was gone play my part for now. I needed the money but right after graduation a nigga was out. Majestic life may have been drugs and shit for the rest of his life but it wasn't mine. Shit, nigga worked hard for that degree.

"Aiight, you sure? The fuck ya'll get locked up for fighting for anyway? Wussup? Ya'll niggas like glue."

No matter how mad Trell was with me right now, I knew he would never betray me like that and go telling my business and shit; especially to a nigga like Majestic cause Trell wasn't cut from that kinda cloth.

"Brother shit." I told him. "We'll be aiight."

"Shit, aiight... but check it. For whatever it's worth, life too fuckin' short my nigga. If ya'll ain't got nobody else ya'll got each other. I can't even hug my brother and tell the nigga I love him right now and that shit fucks with me every singe day. Make that shit right before it's too late."

Majestic was on some bullshit most of the time, but I felt everything he'd just said to me. However, I knew I had to give this shit some time cause Trell is a fucking hot head. "I hear you man. I'll see you at the spot later." I told him before hanging up.

I parked in my usual spot when I got to Kevin's house and hopped out. I hadn't even noticed LeLe sitting inside of her truck in the parking lot until she hopped out. "Unt Unt what are you doing here? You have to go." She tried pushing me back.

I looked at her like she was crazy as fuck. I was confused too cause what the fuck was going on? "Nah sis, what the fuck you doing here?" I scratched my head.

"Kevin reached out to me and I've been dodging him. Today I got enough balls to come and talk to him; so you gotta go. That man's been through enough."

I couldn't even make sense of this situation. "So you ain't mad at me?"

She shrugged and I could tell it made her uncomfortable. "I mean, maybe. It's weird as shit. I don't like it. You're supposed to have a wife and make me some nieces and nephews. You can't do that if you're with a man but the heart wants what the heart wants."

"Man, I don't even know what to say."

"Well don't say anything. Just let me go talk to Kevin and see what he wants. He deserves to be heard. No matter what though, you're my brother and we're family. Family has to stick together just like ya'll stuck by me when I caught my charge." She reached up on her toes to hug me.

I hugged her back. "I really needed those words."

"I'll call you when I leave. You have a graduation to be focused on. Everything will work itself out." She assured me before sending me on my way.

I didn't know how I felt about them linking up and talking and shit but the fact that Kevin even wanted to talk to my sister gave me some kind of hope. Since she was dealing with that. I went and looked a few apartments I scribbled down from Craigslist hoping that I could find one today.

Chapter 6

Leandra 'LeLe' Wells

I took a deep breath before building enough courage to finally walk up to Kevin's door. I know what I said to Leon, but in all honesty I didn't know how I felt about Kevin. Leon doesn't even look gay. From the naked eye nobody would ever think that so I had my mind already set on one thing. Kevin done turned my damn brother out and I didn't like him for that. However, Leon is a grown ass man and it's nothing nobody could just make him do. The rational side of me knew that. I still had on my work clothes since I hadn't gotten a chance to change yet. Before I walked inside Cass called me. I ignored his call and knocked on the door not knowing what to expect.

Taking a deep breath, I had to prepare myself when I heard the door unlocking. I was expecting to see a flamboyant little shit greeting me but much to my surprise it wasn't like that at all. Even with his bruises I could see this man was pretty as shit. He wore a simple white tee with a pair of Tru Religion jeans and some socks. His curly hair was out on top of his head. Although both his eyes were black and blue, I could still see the pretty greens staring right at me. "LeLe?" He asked.

I nod my head and extended my hand to his. "Yes, nice to meet you."

He didn't shake my hand back. Instead, he embraced me in a friendly hug. "I'm sorry. I'm a hugger Hun. It's nice to meet you. Come inside." He welcomed me in.

His place was cozy looking with a very expensive, yet comfortable taste. Made me wonder if he was some kind of decorator or something. "May I sit?" I asked.

He led me to his couch where he had a glass of wine and some simple finger foods on the table. I believe he noticed how uneasy I was. "It's okay. I know this is kind of awkward." He sat down. "I just felt the need to explain myself to at least one of the siblings and express how sorry I am. I never in a million years imagined that something like this would happen." I took a sip of his wine. I could see that the right side of his jaw still looked a little puffy. My hat went off to him cause I wouldn't have been explaining shit had somebody beat me the way Trell beat him.

I sighed. "Listen Kevin, I'm not really here to judge you. Shit happens, it's life."

"Yes, I know, I know. Just allow me to explain. Leon has been hiding me forever and I've played by all of his rules ya know? Its not fun loving somebody who's constantly hiding you and dogging you out because they can't figure out what's going on with themselves."

There was only silence as I listened.

"Now, Leon had made multiple promises to me. That day that I saw Trell, I swear to God I didn't know he was Trell. In all honesty I thought he was Leon and it pissed me off. I guess it was just a build up of him playing mind games with me so when I saw him hugged up with that girl. I lost it. I regret it."

I assumed the girl he was talking about was Abbey, so I didn't even elaborate on that. Abbey knew my brothers were my world and I loved them with everything in me. I'm not even sure if I was mad that they were fucking at this point. It's just the fucked up way she went about it. Don't sit in my face like it's all good and you're being one hundred percent solid when all the while you've probably just got done bouncing on my baby brother's dick. That's not how this was supposed to work.

"Well I can say this, Trell is much different from Leon. Leon is a little more rational while Trell is a hot head ya know? I'm glad you're clearing this up but it doesn't fix the damage that it caused between two brothers. Had you not done what you did; that fight would've never happened and Leon would have had a chance to figure out how he wanted his secret to come out. I'm almost positive that wasn't the way and it made it worse. Because of that, Leon and Trell both got locked up for Leon defending you."

I could tell from the look on his face that he didn't know that part. "Because of me? Wait, I haven't spoken to Leon since that night. I had no idea that he was even locked up." He dropped his face in his hands for a brief second. "Lord, what have I done?"

"Well, yeah, that's what happened and now they aren't talking at all because of it. This is the first time they've never been speaking to each other. They never even had a fight up until now. At least not a physical fight."

"I feel like shit. I didn't mean for any of this to happen. For what it's worth, from the bottom of my heart, I truly apologize and I don't want anyone to think it was his or her fault cause it wasn't. It was my own judgment and I was wrong."

While speaking to him, Cass called me three more times. I knew I had better leave to call him and see what was going on. I don't think I forgot to lock up or anything. I took a sip of the wine and stood up. "Thanks for this conversation Kevin. I mean, I don't know what else to say besides that. There's nothing I can fix. I wasn't even sure about how I truly felt up until speaking to you. Of course I didn't want this for my brother but if you two love each other than who am I to tell you not to?" I shrugged. "I can't say that Trell or even my mom will be as easy going as me but at the end of the day. It's ya'll life."

Kevin gave me a smile and my God. He had some beautiful teeth. "I appreciate you."

I squint my eyes at him. There was one question that I just couldn't hold my tongue anymore on. "Kevin, did your pretty ass turn my brother out? Like what made you want him out of all people?"

"See, that's the thing LeLe." He shook his head with a look of frustration. "I didn't turn Leon out. I would never disrespect a straight man like that. Leon came on to me. He initiated this situation. Did I think he was cute? Yes I did. However, I would've never over stepped those boundaries."

"Wait, he came on to you?" I asked shocked.

"He did."

Whew, this was too much to deal with. Clearly Leon has been battling with himself for a long time. He had to deal with this on his own. "Okay, well thanks for the drinks, the invite and the conversation but I have to run now. I'll be sure to let Leon know we spoke."

He chuckled. "Oh come on LeLe, he knows we're speaking right now. I saw him outside. I just didn't say anything. I don't know what to say. I told him I didn't want to see him anymore because his family will never accept me."

"Okay, you told him that and he still came right? No matter what you said."

"So what are you trying to say?" He asked.

"I think you already know." I told him. "I have to head out. Nice meeting you." I told him before walking out of his apartment. I couldn't say I didn't like Kevin. Truth is, he seemed like a decent guy. This situation wasn't up to me though so there was nothing that I could do.

I immediately called Cass back as soon as I left Kevin's. "Hey Cass."

"Sup baby, where you at?" He asked.

"I'm leaving from handling some family business. Is everything okay? Did I forget to lock up?"

"No, you didn't forget but I do have something I need to show you. Can you meet me at the house?"

I looked at the time first. "Sure, I have some time to spare." I smiled. "I'm coming." Ever since that day he pulled that last stunt Cass had been trying his hardest to get into my good graces. I couldn't say it wasn't working cause in reality, he was such a sweetheart. We'd been good but I refused to fuck him or give him any pussy no matter how bad I wanted to. Before I gave my body to another man, I wanted to know he was truly good for me. I didn't want to get caught up in no soul ties with nobody.

Outside of work and stacking my money, life was straight up boring. I didn't have nobody to have girl talk with outside of Karter and I was getting tired of her black and proud speeches but upon explaining to her the situation with Abbey and how I couldn't take her sister's bullshit no more, she completely understood. My spare time had now been wrapped up into Cass. I called him back to let him know I was heading home to change first but he was totally against it telling me it was cool.

As soon as I made it to his house, I parked and grabbed my purse from the passenger seat. I noticed that Trey's truck was parked out front as well. I hadn't seen much of him but whenever I did it was awkward cause he never had much to say. The man was truly about his money. Most of the time when he was around he was observing. I was starting to think he wasn't as close with Cass as I initially thought he was. He never had much to say to him either; just made his money and went on about his business.

Cass was at the door waiting for me bear chested and wearing a pair of jeans with sock on his feet as he munched down on a green apple. He wore his ice around his neck as well and I could tell he had a fresh tape. He looked damn good per usual. "Even with work clothes on you look good as fuck ma." He pulled me into a bear hug while tickling me.

"Put me down Cass." I laughed while squealing. "Now what's the rush? What's so urgent that I just had to get here?"

He leaned up against the wall staring at me. "Nothing, I just want to see that pretty little face."

I furrowed my brows. "Oh hell no." I chuckled. "I'm outta here."

He stopped me in my tracks. "You bet not." He admired me. "I like what you did with yo hair. So glad you ain't got that damn bun in."

I playfully slapped his arm. "Whatever. Seriously though, what happened? Cause I'm tired and I'm not cooking for you today." I took a seat on the sofa and placed my hand up under my chin looking at him waiting for a response. He walked over to me and pulled me up into a hug.

"Walk with me." He led me out back to hic closed in pool area. The sun was setting and the beautiful orange reddish hue in the sky was breathtaking to me. Being locked away in prison made me appreciate shit like this. Then again it was the smallest things that I realized I enjoyed. Like the birds chirping. The plants, the trees, feeling the rain and everything else. Stuff that people took for granted. You never know how much you appreciate that stuff until you just simply didn't have it anymore. Everyday I learned more things about myself.

"Cass!" I gasped looking at the table he had set up for two. There was a bottle of wine and a whole lobster feast for us. He had the candles going. The warm buttered bread that smelled oh so good. There was fresh tossed salad with all of the mixings. Cucumbers, tomatoes, onions, and bacon bits. Right next to my plate there was a box. "Awww Cass this is beautiful." I beamed placing both of my arms around his neck hugging him. "What's all this for?"

He pulled my chair out to sit down before he took his chair. "Shit ma, a nigga appreciate you that's all. I want you to know that. Even Jazzy's and shit, you hold it down. It's yo cooking that keep that keeps them coming back shorty."

I did enjoy cooking and had been thinking about my life a lot lately. I had made the decision that eventually I wanted to go ahead and open my own restaurant. I knew I could do it. I just didn't know how to break the news to Cass that I wouldn't be working for him forever, but now I just planned to enjoy the moment. "I appreciate that Cass. Matter of fact, I appreciate everything that you've done for me. Seriously I really do. I don't think I would've been able to do any of this without you." It was true, had he not given me that job I'd be fucked up barely making ends meet. Cass paid me well too. I'm a convicted felon, there was nowhere else I could go and make a stack a week.

Because of him, I'd been able to save up damn good and I wasn't broke and wasn't struggling. Because of him, I was able to keep stacking with plans to actually go ahead and open up that restaurant I've been thinking about. I'd then use that revenue to purchase me a home. I didn't know where this thing with Cass in me was going but I would forever be grateful for him. "You would've done it shorty. You got that drive in you. Don't know if it would've happened as quickly but I'm sure you wouldn't have laid down for too long." He took the box and passed it to me. "Open it."

"What is this?" I smiled before opening it and staring down at a iced out Cuban link bracelet with the iced out charms hanging from it that read my name 'LeLe'. "Oh wowww, this is beautiful." I cooed. As bad as I wanted to put it on, I just didn't know if I could accept it. "Cass, why do you buy me all of these things? I don't need this. You could've just given me the money and I would've surely used that to flip it and invest in something."

Out of nowhere, Trey appeared in the doorway holding yet another duffle bag. I swear he got finer every time I saw him. I promise he heard our conversation because when he looked at me I could have sworn he had a slight smile on his face as if he liked my response. Today he wore all black with a black L.A cap on his head. His hairline was taped fresh and his cologne tickled my nose from where he was standing. I was surprised to see he had some ice around his neck today. His eyes adverted from mine to Cass. "Aiight, this everything. I'mma make that drop off and hit yo line later."

Cass nodded his head and gave Trey a pound. "My nigga... you be on it. One of the only niggas I trust with everything when it come to that bread." Cass then looked at me. "This nigga gone get the job done baby."

I watched Trey adjust his gun in the small of his waist. Shit turned me on. I couldn't accuse them of doing shit else besides handling money when it came to the restaurant cause I never saw anything, but my heart told me that there may have been some other shit going on. These niggas were handling way too much money for me. Trey didn't say much. He just walked away with a simple nod of the head.

I watched him walk away and then turned back to Cass waiting for his explanation. "Anything I do for you is cause I can and cause you deserve it. Don't ever question me doing anything for you ma. That shit is a disgrace." He took a sip from his glass. "You special LeLe. You ain't like the rest of these begging ass bitches. Remember that."

I didn't want to argue with him to seem ungrateful or nothing like that. The last thing I wanted to do was kill his ego so I didn't say anything else. I guess he sensed my own frustration. "Look, this don't mean shit aiight? Ion expect shit from you because of this or nothing else that I do for you. We on our own time ma."

"Well thank you." I smiled. He picked the bracelet back up and I allowed him to place it on my wrist. It was so bomb, and heavy too. This wasn't any little girl shit and of course it was shining. I knew he had to pay a grip for this damn bracelet, but still, I would've preferred the money. If Cass knew anything about me then he would know I want a material girl like that. I left that life when Malik left me and Lord knows that man spoiled me.

Chapter 7

Leandra 'LeLe' Wells

Cass wanted to go hang out for a little bit, but I opted to stay inside. That club shit just wasn't the same for me anymore, especially since I didn't drink hard liquor. I barely wanted to drink wine. The last place Malik and me had spent together was inside of the damn club. I just didn't want to. I was expecting Cass to feel a way but he didn't. He only told me he understood. Since he never let me go home, I showered at his place and put on a big shirt and a pair of basketball shorts that I had to tie up in a knot to get them to fit. His big sock barely fit my feet but I was comfortable.

We laid up watching 'Paid In Full' while I ate some cookies-n-cream ice cream. Per usual, Cass was on his phone doing numbers. In the middle of the movie his house phone rang scaring the shit out of me. Like who really still had a house phone now days anyway? "Get that for me ma." He didn't even look up.

I followed the ringing to the kitchen and grabbed the cordless phone. "Hello?"

Silence.

"Hello?" I asked again.

"Let me speak to Poochie." The female demanded.

I frowned. "Poochie? You have the wrong number." I told her.

She hung up.

"Who was that?" Cass asked me.

I shrugged and sat back down. "Some female asking for Poochie. I told her she had the wrong number."

He briefly looked up at me and stared at me without saying anything. He then looked back down to his phone and kept doing what he was doing. After that he walked in the kitchen and came back out with a Corona in his hand. We cuddled up until he dozed off. I had to literally pick myself up from the couch to go and put my ice cream bowl in the sink. I noticed the phone was flashing but it wasn't ringing. I assumed he turned the ringer off when he grabbed his beer. That was weird.

~~~~~~~

The next morning, we woke up and prepared to leave but Cass seemed to have an attitude. "I'm starving." I yawned covering my mouth from my morning breath. Cass was already fully dressed and laughing at me.

"You still have a toothbrush here ma. Don't be scared to use it."

"Whatever." I mumbled and ran off to brush my teeth and wash my face. When I came back, Cass was at the door waiting for me.

"Come on ma. I'mma take you to get a carryout from Arline's and then bring you back to your truck. I gotta make a stop first." He said looking like his whole demeanor had changed.

I grabbed my keys and whatever else I needed so I wouldn't have to come back inside when we got back. "What's wrong?" I asked.

"Nothing." He mumbled walking out to his truck before he locked up. I decided not to ask him shit else cause whatever it was, he clearly didn't want to tell me. We drove to Doral where it was a bunch of nice ass houses. I mean big and pretty houses too. I sat quietly until we pulled in front a nice two-story home with the most beautiful landscaping that I'd ever seed. There were even palm trees in the front that were clearly planted there. There was a baby Benz in the front and another foreign whip. It was a Bentley, and it looked like the same exact one the girl CoCo had been driving that day. "Stay right here." He told me.

I'm not sure why he was telling me that cause I wasn't going anywhere anyway. This was his run, not mine. I was shocked however to see him pull out a key and let himself in. I sat back and adjusted the air to blow in my face before scrolling my phone until he decided to come back out. It took all about 30 minutes before he mad his way back to the car and when he did, he had visible scratches on his hands and looked like he'd been playing tug of war or something. "What the fuck happened to you?" I frowned.

He backed out and pulled off without even looking at me. "Had to fix some shit. Didn't think it was gone be so much trouble but I'll call my guy to come fix it."

See, I could already tell Cass thought he could get one over on me. He must have felt me staring at the side of his face. He turned the music down. "Wussup ma?"

"Who lives there? Cause wasn't that the girl CoCo's car parked out front? I remember that car from the night you took me to the hospital."

He smirked. "Come on shorty. That bitch ain't the only one with a Bentley. This is Miami. you know how many muhfuckas got the same Bentley? That's one of the properties that I own."

"Oh okay." Was all that I said.

The next stop was to Arline's where I ordered me some corn beef hash, cheese eggs, grits and buttered toast with a fruit punch flop. Cass decided he wanted an omelet, which made me realize he always ordered breakfast omelets. Didn't matter where we ate for breakfast, that's what it was going to be. His phone blew up the entire time he was taking me to my car and the more it rang, the more frustrated he became. I knew it was a bitch. I wasn't mad at him though cause we weren't exclusive and as far as I'm concerned he was pursuing me and in these moments I couldn't tell him not to talk to bitches.

Trey was walking around from the back of Cass's house when we pulled up. He was empty handed. He gave Trey a nod of the head. "I guess I'll call you later on?" I ask with a tilt of the head. "I mean, it seems like you're already having a pretty interesting day and I would hate to intervene with that."

He simply shook his head. "No matter what kind of day I'm having ma. That'll never effect what kind of man I'm supposed to be to you." He assured me. I couldn't say that Cass was a bad dude. Even if he was, he had a hell of a way covering it up cause he did and said all the right things. He reached over and gave me a kiss on the lips. I don't know why I hesitated. Maybe it was the creepy feeling of Trey watching us. Or wasn't he? I'm not sure, maybe it was just his presence alone. "I'll call you later. Go do some girly shit today with ya partna's them. You work hard ma. You deserve it."

I nod my head and gave him a sly smile before walking away. I stood in the driveway and waved as he pulled off. When he was gone, I turned around and caught Trey staring at me. Well, the charm bracelet that dangled on my arm. He gave me a disapproving look. Trey was starting to piss me the fuck off. I tossed my bags in my trunk and stomped over to him shielding the sun out of my face. "What's your fucking problem with me Trey?" I sassed.

He never changed his demeanor when he looked at me. Even with me being confrontational. "You don't need to be drawing that kind of attention to yo'self ma." He nod toward the bracelet. I looked down at it. I didn't see what the big deal was. I didn't plan on wearing it all the time anyway. Trey didn't give me a chance to say anything else. He pulled off leaving me where I stood.

I didn't know what the fuck his problem was but he was starting to piss me off with this love hate type of relationship shit we had with each other. Like he didn't fuck with me like that, but at the same time he was always tryna spit some game to me about something. I drove in silence wondering what it was about him. Hell, I wondered what was going on with Cass as well cause his ass was hiding something. That's exactly why I scribbled down that address. I was going back to get some answers. I knew damn well that was CoCo's car in the driveway.

I refused to be around here giving my heart to a nigga not even knowing who he truly was. If he was hiding something. I needed to know. Like I've been saying. I'm not going back to jail 'over' a nigga cause I'm fighting with bitches, and I'm not going back to jail 'for' a nigga. Nothing was worth my freedom. I almost picked up my phone to call Abbey and vent but, I was still too pissed with her ass.

When I pulled up in front of my house, I was shocked to see my mama's car home since I expected her to be at the hospital. I had one foot in the door before I noticed her sitting on the couch wiping her tears. "What's wrong with you?" I frowned.

"Leon is moving out LeLe. Did you know that? And this rumor about him. It's true. I can feel it."

I tossed my coat over the coat rack and sat next to her. "How do you know?"

She grabbed a napkin blowing away the snot from her nose. "Cause I just do. That's my child. I birthed him. It's true. I knew that when I looked him in the eyes." I gently placed my hand on top of hers to comfort her immediately regretting it. Fuck, I forgot to take the damn bracelet off. "LeLe what the fuck is that? Where did you get that? And don't tell me no fucking restaurant money either." She grabbed my wrist examining it.

"It's not a big deal ma. I got it from a friend of mine. Actually my Boss."

"Don't tell me this isn't a big deal. I'm from the streets. I just look like this. You kids think ya'll got it all figured out but in reality ya'll still got milk around ya'll mouth. The same way Leon and Trell think I haven't noticed the money they've been coming in here with. Now that man may pay you good money but when a man gives you something like this hunny… that shit comes with a price. Ain't nothing for free."

"Ma…"

She cut me off. "Ma, nothing LeLe. You grown so I can't tell you what to do but I'm telling you this. This little gift came from more than just food chain money. If your black ass goes back to jail, you're on your own this time. I can promise you that. I'm not running down there, nor am I busting my ass to send you no money."

She didn't even give me a chance to respond. She just got up and walked away with an attitude. She had too many other problems. I didn't want her worrying about mine too.

Chapter 8

Kimberly 'Kim' Laws

Karter hadn't even been fresh out the hospital for a good 48 hours before the bullshit was starting. The entire fucking hospital incident was a mess. Obviously there was some shit that Karter and her fiancé Emily needed to discuss after Emily realized that Karter's own family didn't know shit about her. The nerve of her ass around here giving power to the people speeches and she's got a whole blonde head woman and a little baby with blue eyes. Now, Barbie is beautiful and wasn't no denying that. However, I didn't like this everybody wanted to be perfect but call Kim out on her shit type of ordeal.

It was a little past midnight and I couldn't sleep, so I left Karter's guest bedroom where I shared a room with Abbey and came to the kitchen to pour me a bowl of cereal. I liked being alone now days. My mama walked in the kitchen dressed down in her pajamas to come and find her something to drink. I had barely said two words to her ass and vice versa. One look at me and she gave me a phony smile. "What you doing up Kimberly? Couldn't sleep?" She asked.

I rolled my eyes in the back of my head. "Oh please, don't come in here being phony. You don't even like me nor do you care about why I'm up." I munched hard on my Froot Loops and continued to mind my business.

"You sound silly as hell Kim. You're my daughter so I don't know why you seem to think I don't love you."

"Had I had a child, would you have come? I live twenty minutes away from you and you drove three hours away for Karter." She looked at me like I was crazy. "My point exactly." She needed to get out of my presence cause she was making me lose my appetite.

"Had you allowed me and not given me any slick ass slide comments, or not try to bash my husband every chance you got then maybe it would be different."

"I hope his ass burns in hell." I mumbled.

She sucked her teeth. "See, this is what I'm talking about."

I left that subject well enough alone. I didn't need to beat her up anymore than she was being beat up realizing that her perfect little baby girl Karter wasn't so perfect after all. Or maybe I would have a little fun with this. "How does it feel ma? To know your little perfect baby girl isn't so perfect after all? Here she was preaching to us all. Meanwhile, she's living in this big ass house with a black nanny. Her fiancé is an attorney and practically rich. Not to mention she's gay as fuck. Or maybe she ain't really gay. Maybe, she settled for what she knew would provide for her for the rest of her life. Karter never had to work for shit. I knew she couldn't get out here in this jungle and survive on her own. You and me both know it."

She stood in front of me and furrowed her brows trying not to speak too loudly. Her lips were balled up when she spoke to me. You know, how black mamas did when they were trying to scare their child. "Now you listen here you little evil winch. The only reason I haven't slapped the taste out of your mouth is cause I know I'll fuck you up something bad if I put my hands on you. You better learn to respect me."

I wanted to slap her hand from my face, but I didn't. I just looked at her like I smelled a piece of shit. I was starting to hate her ass.

"Now I don't give a shit what Karter did, or what she's doing. What she has going on ain't bothering you or interrupting your bitter ass life so you might wanna fall back. Of course I love my kids through it all." She spat. "When I found out I was pregnant, I prayed for a daughter and God blessed me with two. What I didn't ask for was the fucking Bride of Chucky with your evil ass."

"Trust and believe my demons started in your house a long time ago."

"Shhhhh." Karter walked in wearing her robe looking like she'd been crying all night. Hell, Emily hadn't said one word to her since we left the hospital. She felt as though Karter was ashamed of her. "Why must ya'll do this here and right now? You'll wake Emily and the baby."

"Sorry." My mama apologized without looking at her cause she was still to focused on gawking at me.

"If not now then when Karter? Cause I'm getting real sick of this. Shit, Emily may just need to hear this. Maybe she'll feel connected to the family since you hid her for so long."

Karter dropped her eyes and shook her head.

"Leave her alone Kim." My mama warned.

"Well you leave me alone."

"Don't talk to mama like that Kim." Karter snapped.

"Easy for you to take up for her. Hell, she believes anything you tell her. She wont even believe when I tell her that her nasty ass husband sexually abused me."

Karter gasped as her hand flew up to her mouth. "Ma… is that true?"

My mama looked to Karter like she had no right to ask her that. "Hell no, she's just looking for attention."

Karter looked from me to my mama before she came and stood next to me. "I believe Kim. She's my sister and I don't think she has no reason to lie about something like that. That's a very serious accusation. I don't care how messed up she is. Maybe that's the reason why."

"How dare ya'll try to get me in here to gang up on me. What kind of shit is this? I drove all these ways to be supportive and you get in here and change on me because of Kim and her lies?"

There were faded footsteps coming toward the kitchen that got closer. Emily stood there as tall as a damn female basketball player. I couldn't deny the fact that she was pretty as hell. "Is everything okay?" She asked looking concerned for us all. "I heard some bickering."

"Go back to bed Emily. It's just family issues." Karter told her trying to push her away. Emily wouldn't budge.

"Ahh I see, and I'm not family right Karter? Because I think you made that very clear."

"Ha!" I blurted. "Emily, you don't want to be a part of this dysfunction. Trust me."

Abbey walked in the kitchen rubbing her eyes. "Shut up Kim. What's the fuss about?"

At this point we were all in a stare down with one another. "I mean, besides the fact that my mama doesn't believe her husband constantly raped me. Karter actually believes me, and Emily is feeling like she's not family since Karter been on her black is power shit and hid the fact that she has a white fiancé, a black nanny, and a blue-eyed baby." I updated her.

Abbey's eyes got so big when she looked at me. "Wait a minute. You were raped Kim?"

"She's a damn lie." Her mama snapped.

"Jesus Christ, this is a goddamn circus." Karter placed one hand on her forehead.

"Why did you hide me Karter?" Emily asked with hurt in her eyes. "Did I not do enough for you? Is any of this even real? The life, the baby? You were so sure when we did that artificial insemination that this is what you wanted." She then looked to us. "I want you women to know. I wanted to meet you all but it was Karter who kept you away. She assured me it had nothing to do with me and everything to do with you."

Abbey fold her arms across her chest. "Karter, I just don't think you have to explain yourself."

I knew Karter's crybaby ass was going to cry when I saw her lips quivering. Yep, the tears were falling. "Emily I… I just… you have no idea what it's like because we come from two totally different worlds. I just wanted to protect you that's all. I never initially tried to hide you. But that's not it. I have my own struggles as well."

Emily may have been a white girl, but she wasn't budging on those tears. She wanted answers.

"You don't understand. The life you give me. This entire lifestyle… it just… I don't even know how to say this. The more I'm up here around you, your family and friends, your colleagues, the more white I feel. The less intact I feel with my own roots. Sometimes I feel as though I'm losing myself in order to love you. I'm a black woman and I constantly have to remind myself that black is beautiful no matter how we may be living up here. You don't even have black friends Emily. Not one. So maybe I was ashamed, but that doesn't mean I don't love you." She cried. "There, I said it."

Abbey and me both walked over to console Karter. No matter what I said, no matter how much I despised her because of her not defending me in our home when we were growing up; she's still my twin sister.

"Well, hell, you act like we're racist or something Karter." My mama added in her two cents. "Cause you never said nothing about having a white woman, hell, you never said you were a lesbian. I have a mixed grandchild in there from semen of a man you don't even know. If that ain't some white shit I don't know what is."

"This is exactly why I didn't tell you." Karter wiped her eyes. "Racist or not, that comment you made was of pure ignorance cause it's not only white people who does that."

"It's really not." Abbey agreed.

"You know babe. Before today, I was so sure about us but obviously there's a lot we need to talk about. Her face was now turning beet red, so I knew she wanted to cry.

"I'm sorry for hurting you Em... you've been nothing but good to me." Karter told her.

"Now see, why is that so hard to do?" I looked to my mama. "You should take notes. Why is it so hard for you to apologize to me for being a horrible mother to me?"

"You know what? That's it!" She rushed me like a bull slapping the shit out of me opting for Emily to immediately grab her while Abbey grabbed me. "After today I officially disown your ungrateful ass!" She tried to pull away from Emily but white girl wasn't having it. Abbey held me back and if it wasn't for that I would've surely fucked my mama up.

My face stung so badly as the tears immediately welled up in my eyes. "I DON'T GIVE A FUCK IF YOU DISOWN ME! YOU BEEN DID THAT!"

"Kim! It's not even worth it! Stop!" Abbey tried to control me.

"NO!" I cried. "FUCK THAT! FUCK HER!"

Meanwhile, Karter's emotional ass stood there crying looking at this bullshit. This wasn't how this trip was supposed to go at all. This was actually supposed to be a happy time. "Babe! Go upstairs now!" Emily told her. "You just had our daughter, this is too much for you right now!"

Karter looked back and forth from us all. "But… this… is my family Emily."

Emily nod her head. "I understand. Just go, I'll handle it."

The baby started crying and Karter didn't have a choice besides to run upstairs.

"You can let me go Emily!" My mama squealed. "I won't touch her! I'm out of here fuck this! I will not be disrespected!"

I stared at her and shook my head as the tears fell. "Why can't you believe me mama? Why can't you just love me?" I broke down.

She gave me one disgusting look. "Not as long as you try to tarnish my husband." She snapped. "Ya'll grown now and mama gotta have a life too." She stormed away to pack her bags.

"Damn." Emily mumbled.

Abbey held on to me hugging me real tight. "I'm so sorry Kim. I did not know it was this bad. I'm soooo sorry." She cried with me.

At this point, I didn't even want to stay anymore my damn self, but I knew Abbey wouldn't leave. Emily walked over to us both and placed her hand on my shoulder. "Just get some rest tonight okay? Let's try to figure this out in the morning."

She was right cause this had been one long ass night. As far as I was concerned, my mama was dead to me. DEAD!

Chapter 9

Leon Wells

After days of searching, I found a decent lil apartment in Aventura. A simple one bedroom with a small living room and a kitchen, that's all I needed. I drug LeLe with me in the process since I didn't have nobody else. I had to wait until she got off work though to have her to come and finalize everything with me. I still hadn't run into Trell since the day I saw him at the house but I knew could avoid each other too long. Eventually we had to man up and handle up. Whatever it was gone be is what it was gone be.

"This is niceeeee." LeLe walked around looking at the place. "You gotta let me decorate for you cause I know you don't know what the hell you doing." She teased.

I leaned up against the wall counting some money. "Yeah, I bet. I don't have time to go do all of that anyway."

She eyeballed the money but didn't say anything. LeLe tried not to say much but I knew she wasn't a fool. Besides, I loved my sister way too much to put her in a bind. I'd never do no flaw shit around her or with her that could get her in trouble and taken away again. "Have you spoken to Kevin?" She asked.

I popped my head up and stopped counting. I hadn't spoken to him. I tried to push him out of my mind the majority of the time. I wanted to make up with my brother first cause when and 'if' Kevin ever came back around I wanted shit to be right this time. I didn't want to hide him or keep doing shit to hurt him cause he's a good person overall. "Nah, but only time will tell." I told her. "Look LeLe, I wanna thank you for everything aiight? I appreciate you being hear. I appreciate you trying to have a open mind, allat."

She smiled at me looking like the prettiest girl in the world. "I'm my brother's keeper for sure." She told me looking like she had something else she wanted to say to me.

"What it is?" I asked. "You can ask me whatever, just don't ask me shit about my intimate life. That's a conversation you and me will never have."

She rolled her eyes. "I would never... trust me. I just want to know. Do you know somebody named Poochie?" She asked.

I didn't know if she was smoking crack or what, but the shit threw me for a loop. "You're fuckin' with me right?"

"No." She replied and I knew she was serious.

"How is it you work for the nigga and don't even know who he is?" I questioned. "I never did like the idea of her running around with him but she swore they were only kicking it and that's it. Honestly, I didn't even know Cass and Poochie was the same person at first. We knew Majestic worked for a nigga named Poochie, and we worked for Majestic. I found out by default that Poochie and Cass was the same person. But still, I was expecting LeLe to know that.

I noticed the way she tensed up. "What the fuck is he hiding then?" She frowned. "You know, somebody called his house and asked for somebody named Poochie and I told her she had the wrong number. He didn't correct me so what the hell is he hiding?"

"Shit, besides he one of the biggest drug dealers pushing dope out of Miami? don't shit move without Poochie saying so. That's what the fuck he's hiding. What the fuck you was doing answering the nigga phone LeLe? You fuckin' with him like that?"

"Nah." She said too quickly. I knew she was lying. Had to be cause why else was she so interested?

"Don't lie to me."

She sighed. "He was pursuing me Leon, and yes we were kicking it." I noticed her eyes water up. "So that means that Trey, his right hand man... he's pushing weight too?"

"Nobody knows shit about that nigga. He don't talk to nobody like that. He does his own thing LeLe. I mean, if you ain't fuckin' with that nigga like that than none of this should even matter."

Her breathing became slow and heavy as she took a seat and dropped her face in the palm of both her hands. "I can't believe he lied to me." She mumbled. "He's had me around him openly knowing that I couldn't afford to be around him. What of the Feds watching that nigga? Anything could be going on with him and I don't need to be an accessory for no fucking body. Leon are you sure?" She asked looking at me again.

"I think I'm almost positive sis. I mean, you can do your own investigation if it makes you feel better. I'm just sayin'." I shrugged.

"Do you know my entire life since I've been home had been built around this man? He saved me when nobody else could do it. Do you know how much he's paying me to even work for him?" She asked.

"I can imagine, shit, he got it."

I didn't like her feeling so distraught over this nigga. "Look, just keep it professional LeLe. Go to work, get ya money, and stay the fuck away from that nigga. If the stories they say about him are true, he's dangerous as fuck. Trell and me may not be seeing eye-to-eye but at the end of the day we'll go in the ground or to the jail about you." I let her know. LeLe is one of the strongest females that I know. I admired her even when she didn't think I did, so I knew she would be okay.

"I know." She sighed and stood up. "Take me back to my truck please. I need to go home."

I grabbed my keys and locked up my lil spot before we headed out. I had really been neglecting my stomach for the past few days by barely eating. I just munched on lil shit here and there but I stopped to Popeye's and grabbed me a spicy chicken sandwich on the way back to the hood to take LeLe to her truck. It was parked right where we left it in the driveway in front of the house. "I heard George came home today."

She nod her head staring out of the window. "He did."

"Mama been going to Bingo?" He asked.

"Nah ion think so." She told me. "I don't think nobody has to worry about that no more. His near death experience scared the shit out of her. You should go inside and see him."

I didn't plan on getting out at first but it would've been selfish of me not to go inside and at least see the man who took care of me the majority of my life. I know my mama told him everything cause her ass couldn't hold water. It wouldn't be like her to not have said shit. I followed LeLe in the house and was glad to see my mama on the couch balled up sleeping with a throw blanket over her. "Shhh. Don't wake her up." LeLe held one finger to her mouth. "I'm not in the mood to hear her shit."

"You and me both." I told her.

In the back room, George lay there on his back slightly sitting up watching television. Although he had a shirt on, we could tell he had gauze underneath that covering his wound. Looked like he'd lost a few pounds as well. When he saw us both, he smiled and winked his eye at us. I knew he could probably talk but I didn't want to make him talk much. He looked so weak. I just wanted him to heal. I hated seeing my main man like this. "How you feeling old man?" I asked him standing next to him.

He only looked at me and nod his head before responding in a slight whisper. "I'm okay. Can't keep a old man down too long." He grabbed my hand and squeezed it. "I love you son. No matter what."

Damn, he was about to have me all choked up cause he just didn't know what that meant to me right now to hear him say that. I'm glad he wasn't looking at me with disgust or like less of a man. I'm still the same person and I wish everybody would realize that. "I love you too old man."

"Don't you worry about nobody else. As long as you're happy." He told me before focusing back on the television. "Can't wait to get up and moving around so I can get a lot of things straight around here."

I didn't say much after that but I wasn't surprised that George had my back. We may not have appreciated him growing up cause we wasn't too fond of him regulating on us, but in the end, he always had our backs. Just like he had LeLe's when she got locked up and still till this very day. I gave him a simple pat on the shoulder and walked out letting him continue to rest. I had to piss so I rushed to the bathroom and washed my hands when I was finished, which gave LeLe a few minutes to chop it up with him.

We walked out at the same time and saw that our mama wasn't on the couch no more. Instead, she was out on the porch smoking. "What you doing with that cancer stick? Thought you stopped smoking?" LeLe frowned fanning the smoke from her face.

She looked at us both with sadness in her eyes. "Yeah, well when your kids driving you to worry like ya'll worrying me this is what it comes down to." She looked me up and down. "So it's official huh? You moved out?"

"You drove me to that. I can't stay under the roof with ya'll judging me and looking at me like a walking piece of shit ma. That's not gone work."

"Boy, I'm ya mama. I'mma love you regardless. Even when it hurts." She said blowing another ring of smoke.

Again, LeLe balled her face up and fanned the smoke from our face. "Well what did I do to you?" She asked.

"Besides hide shit and run around here with dope boys? I'm worried sick about you LeLe. If you go to jail again that'll just kill me. Do you know that's a terrible feeling for a mother to have her child locked up like a caged animal and there's absolutely nothing I can do about it?"

LeLe sighed. "Ma, go see about George. He's wide-awake. Nothing is going to happen to me." She kissed her cheek and walked to her truck. I kissed her cheek and did the same leaving her staring at us both.

As we both pulled off to go our separate ways, Trell was pulling up. I watched LeLe roll down her window and say a few words to him before she zoomed down the street. On the other hand, he didn't even look my way. I mean, it was cool, then again that shit hurt. Big time.

Chapter 10

Leandra 'LeLe' Wells

I sat outside the house staring at the Bentley truck debating on if should even knock or not. I had some questions that I needed answers to and this was going to be where I got the answers. "Fuck it." I mumbled to myself ignoring all of Cass's calls. I tucked my phone in the pocket of my jeans and knocked on the door. I knew somebody was home cause all the lights were on. Within a few seconds the door was opening and CoCo was staring at me holding a small gun to her side.

"Shit." She mumbled. "You scared the fuck out of me? What are you doing at my house? Did Poochie send you to spy on me?" She squinted.

"Um no." I threw my hands up. "It's just me." I looked around behind me. "Can I come in?"

She used one hand pulling me inside locking the door behind us. She didn't say another word. Just led me the kitchen where she turned on another bright light and looked at me. It was now I could see the black eye and busted lip she wore. "What do you want? Besides to ask me questions about Poochie?" I frowned and she picked up on my look. "Well, why else are you here? You ain't the first and won't be the last."

"I'm not fucking the nigga if that's what you're thinking." I let her know. "What happened to your face?" I asked. Here she was put up in this big ass house, expensive cars, iced out, and wearing a bruised eye and busted lip.

"Humph. Guess you haven't felt the wrath of Poochie huh?" She smirked. "From the first day I saw you. I knew you'd eventually end up finding me. The question I'll ask again. What do you want?"

"CoCo, who exactly are you to Cass?"

She laughed. I didn't know what was so funny. "Open those big pretty eyes girl. To Cass, I'm his child's mother. To Poochie, I'm just another bitch on the streets."

"Wait, so whatever I heard about him is probably true then?" I nibbled on my bottom lip.

"Everything you heard about him is true. Believe me." She snapped her fingers. "You gotta say what you gotta say and get out of here. He catches you here then you and me both get fucked up. I can't afford that. You see this lifestyle? It looks nice but all this shit comes with a price girl."

I wanted to just pick my whole face up off the floor. "Can I ask why you allowing him to hide you? Like, the nigga says he doesn't have a girl or any kids."

"Oh please. I don't mind him hiding me. I don't want nobody knowing I'm connected to him to that extent. If shit goes sour and niggas come looking for him, my son and me are vulnerable. It's best this way. He keeps me dripped in Gucci and Gold to put up with his lifestyle."

"Does accepting black eyes come with that?" I questioned. "I wasn't even trying to be funny. That was a real question."

"Look, don't worry about me. You just watch yourself aiight? I'm warning you like my brother Trey tried to warn me. I didn't listen and now the nigga don't fuck with me at all. He sends gifts for his nephew but that's about it. " She started walking to the door. "You gotta go."

I could see in her face and hear it in her voice that she was really uncomfortable with me being here. My mind was made up. I would continue to cook at Jazzy's but I was done with Cass. Whatever he was looking for out of me just couldn't happen. I wanted to ask her more but I didn't want to push it. "Thank you, for whatever it's worth."

She sighed and held the door. "Look, I don't give a shit about Poochie's ass. He provides the lifestyle that I need and even if he didn't. He will never let me leave him because of our son. You don't gotta even get involved with him like that. Stop fucking with that nigga before his feelings gets all the way involved cause if he does… he's not letting you go that easy. He likes having control." She looked out to my truck. "I hope that shit is in your name."

"It is." I told her.

"Good." She replied. "Goodnight." She closed the door in my face and left me to walk to the truck with a lot of shit on my mind.

I drove all the way home in silence. I just needed to think. I needed to put my own play in motion and start working on my own restaurant. I felt like shit cause deep down inside I really felt as though the hole I felt in my heart was slowly coming to a closure. Obviously that wasn't true. The few conversations Trey and I did have played in my mind over and over. Trey said a few things that I always seemed to overlook. Maybe I didn't want anything or anybody to ruin what I may have thought could become a fairytale. Cass came in like a knight and shining armor and in reality, he's a big ass liar. There was no way he could care about me because he lied to me about his situation, knowing my situation.

I locked the door on my truck and hopped out to walk inside. Trell was sitting on the porch smoking a joint. "Where you been?" He asked.

"With Leon." I told him. He put the joint out while he spoke to me. He knew damn well I didn't like that shit. So far, going to my probation officer, my piss always came back clean and I didn't want to risk anything else. "He got his own place."

Trell leaned back in the chair staring out at the cars. "You heard from Abbey?" He asked ignoring what I said about Leon.

"No. I don't want to talk to her ass right now and you either to be honest."

"Yo, what's your real problem LeLe?"

"First of all Trell, you my brother, but I'm sorry... you ain't shit and you know you ain't shit. How many other bitches were you fucking besides Abbey?"

Silence.

"Yeah, I thought so. You think I want you fucking with my friend knowing you'd dog her out and I'll have to hide it and act like I don't know shit cause you're my brother?" I sighed. "On top of that she knew better, she broke the girl code. What if ya'll were to get serious and it doesn't work? That shit is just too messy for me. There's your answer."

Trell's little fine ass just stared at me like he was reading me. I really liked his new look with the dreads gone. It made him even more handsome. "You can talk about how many bitches I was fucking; the real question is how many do I actually give a fuck about? Cause right about now it's none to one."

I had my face twisted all the fuck up. "Are you sitting here telling me that you actually care about Abbey in that kind of way?"

He shrugged and wiped his hands down his face. "Ion know what I'm saying and to be honest with you, seems like the shit don't even matter cause she wont even talk to me at all. Before you go hollerin' bout that value of a friendship shit, just remember that. She fighting her own heart just to be loyal to you." He told me.

I thought about Leon's situation. "Well if you want to put it that way, that's the same thing Leon is doing because of you."

Silence.

I knew he didn't want to talk to me about Leon cause he was still hurt so I didn't bother to push it. "I'm going to shower and go to bed." I told him walking in the dark house as I crept to my room to get everything I needed to shower. I placed my phone on the charger in my room in the meantime and when I came back out. I had a few missed calls from Cass and two from Karter. I didn't plan on calling Cass back, so I called Karter instead but she didn't pick up the phone. Next I checked my messages realizing that I had picture mail from Karter. Staring back at me was a picture of a beautiful blue-eyed baby girl that didn't have a lick of melanin in her skin. She actually looked like Karter, the spitting image so I knew it had to be the baby. Under the picture was a message: *We need to talk.*

I thought the same thing as I looked at the picture again. I knew I wasn't a genius or no shit like that but this baby looked mighty damn white to me. I shot her back a text letting her know I was going to call her tomorrow before laying down and putting my phone on silent.

Chapter 11

Abbey Daniels

After being in Orlando for almost a week it was finally time to go. This was the last and final day and I hated it had to come to an end cause despite everything that had happened, Kim and me really did enjoy the baby. She was so precious. I hadn't been feeling too well, but at the same time I also needed to get back to work and back to my real life. I had been playing therapist to Emily and Karter too. I couldn't say that I didn't like Emily cause in reality she end up being a cool ass white girl and she really did love Karter.

It was Karter the one having the issue of finding balance and acceptance. In reality, she was indeed ashamed and if she didn't get it together she was going to confuse Barbie when she got older. Let's not even talk about poor Kim. I tried to keep her close and keep my eyes on her but in the bathroom behind those closed doors; I had no control over what she did. I wanted to speak to Karter about Kim's snorting issue but now just wasn't the time. They both had been on edge after the ordeal with their mama. Karter had been crying for days behind it. She was just too embarrassed.

I hopped in the shower and got myself together while Kim and Karter sat out by the pool. The baby was upstairs with Emily and Kim smoked a joint while allowing her feet to dangle in the pool. She was already packed up and ready to go. After showering, I locked the room door and sat on the bed to scroll my Instagram account. Ironically a picture of Trell popped up first. He'd been in the strip club last night and him and his boys looked like they had a good time. I missed him so much but his young ass had to stay away from me.

I hurriedly got off before I ended up calling his ass. I needed to have a talk with LeLe when I got back in town. I didn't care how mad she was. I needed to update her on a lot of shit and I needed her to know she didn't have to worry about Trell and me anymore. I can't even front and say I didn't miss the excitement or the rush he gave me. In a normal day of my basic ass life, he could come around and make it exciting with his bullshit. Not to mention, I needed some dick in the worst way.

I rummaged through my bag and put on a pair of black tights with a pullover hoodie. I then went to the mirror and brushed my hair into a ponytail slicked back and hanging low before putting on my big-hooped earrings. I wanted to see the baby before I went outside to join Kim and Karter but Emily was sleeping with the baby lying on her chest and I didn't want to wake them. Making my way back down the stairs, I got a whiff of Karter and Kim's conversations since the sliding door was cracked. I was glad they were having a heart-to-heart and that made me not even want to intervene. I decided to sit in the living room and pull out my phone to do some reading in my kindle app.

They were so engulfed in their conversation that they hadn't even noticed me and at first I wasn't even paying attention until I heard Kim start to cry. "My life is fucked up Karter. You don't even understand. I hated you for that shit. I hated the fact that you never said shit to take up for me."

"I honestly didn't know Kim. I thought you worked because you just liked your own money when we were growing up. I had no idea that they just wouldn't do anything for you. I didn't even know Brian was doing that to you. I would've killed him. I swear." She sniffed. "For whatever it's worth I'm sorry. I really am. I don't care what mama believes. I believe you Kim."

Now my antennas were up. I was so glad they were having this conversation.

"You know, that's where all of my problems started Karter. Right there in that fucked up house. From there it just went down." Kim told her.

"But it'll get better Queen." Karter assured her.

Kim shook her head and wiped her tears. "Nah Karter, it goes deeper than this. I've been wanting to talk to you and get some stuff off my chest but you have to promise me that it stays right here."

"I promise." She told her.

"Well, about two years ago I started sniffing coke and…"

"You what?!" Karter blurted. "No Kim! No! That is not acceptable! You have to stop doing that shit. You have to."

"Karter…" She said sucking her teeth. "Sit back down and just listen." She continued. "Besides having my other issues. There's something else that led me to do that. It had something to do with Malik." She whispered.

"Malik?" Karter asked. "What does he have to do with this?"

"He was mine first Karter." Kim admitted.

My heart dropped. I know damn well she didn't just say Malik was her man.

"What?" Karter asked sounding confused.

"It's just what I said. We met first Karter. We used to fuck on the low but he made me promise not to tell nobody cause he claimed he didn't want people in his business. Then he met LeLe and it was over for me. He flaunted her, he wife her when he wouldn't even wife me. I never said shit about it cause he made me swear I wouldn't. I was just a fuck." She sniffed.

Oh hell Naw. I thought to myself. This was just too much. My mind went back to the night Malik proposed to LeLe. Kim was the only one not too enthused about it. Shit was starting to make sense.

"Kim. I don't think I want to know anymore." Karter told her. "I'm starting to feel dizzy cause where is this going?"

"The night Malik died Karter…" Kim sighed.

Karter stood up. "Kim! Stop right now!" She closed her ears. "I don't want to hear it! Just stop! Whatever it is keep it to yourself! Please."

I didn't even realize that I was shaking. I surely didn't know I had tears in my eyes until I felt the warm water on my face when I walked out the sliding door with my face balled up. "Nah spill it! What happened Kim?

What about the night Malik died… huh?" I had my fist balled up in her face.

At this point, Kim looked hopeless. She didn't even try to hide her tears or none of that. She just looked defeated. "It was me Abbey." The snot trickled from her nose she cried so hard. "I was hurt. I was so jealous. Like, how could he just dog me out like that? I spiked the drinks. I just wanted to hurt them. I didn't want anybody to die! I didn't mean it! I swearrr! I wasn't in my right frame of mind. I was so high I didn't remember!"

Whap!

Before I knew it, I was leaping on top of Kim fucking her ass up while she balled up in a fetal position crying and shaking while trying to protect her face. "You stupid bitch!" I balled out on her while Karter just screamed trying to break it up. "You stupid fucking bitch! That man loss his life! You caused LeLe to go to prison and do that time feeling guilty that she killed that man! It was cause of you Kim? Really?!"

I was so goddamn mad it took for me to see blood for me to stop. Her nose and mouth were both leaking something terrible as she cried and shook. I loved my friend but she fucked up big time. I grabbed her by her shirt ready to hit her again, but looking into her eyes. I saw a hurt, fucked up individual who needed help. I wrapped both my arms around her and squeezed her tight. "Why Kim! Whyyy!" I cried. "You could've just talk to me! You had people to talk to! This shit didn't have to be like this!"

For the next ten minutes the only sounds that could be heard was low sobbing from the three of us as Karter and me both held on to Kim. I tried to fix everything, I couldn't fix this. "You're going to have to admit to Majestic and Kim both what you did Kim." I told her. "Majestic hates LeLe for what happened to his brother. I can see right through that front he tries to put on."

Kim sniffed. "I'm finding myself caring for him when I never wanted to. It was just about sex but now I have to tell him. That's like signing my own death certificate." She admitted.

"Wait, you're fucking Majestic?" Karter asked confused.

Kim gave her a simple head nod.

"Wow Kim, is there anything else?" She asked.

Kim shook her head 'no'.

"I'm just sorry about everything. I can't take it back. I want to get better. I don't want to live with these demons no more. I'm going to admit my wrongs and deal with whatever comes to me but I'm asking you both to please let me do it on my time. Soon."

"I can't promise you that." I told her. "LeLe deserves to know the truth." I told her.

Silence filled the air while we all were deep in our own thoughts. Why the fuck did I have to be the one to know about the secrets? This was one I truly wished I didn't know. I know what Kim did was fucked up but I didn't want her to die because of it. She needed help, so what were we supposed to do? Help her? Like how? I didn't even know where to start.

There was nothing else spoken between us. The tension was way too thick. Even on the road heading back home there was nothing said. When I dropped Kim off home it was an awkward silence. I think we all just needed some time to figure a lot of shit out. Almost to my house, I called LeLe to see if she would pick up. She didn't. maybe I was glad that she didn't pick up either.

I was too exhausted at this point. After I grabbed my bags and went inside of the house I showered again and poured me a glass of wine. I grabbed my throw blanket and balled up on the couch wiping my own tears. I hated being put in fucked up positions. I hated all the shit that was happening was happening as well. About fifteen minutes later there was a knock on my door so I got up to check it.

Trell was standing there waiting for me to open the door. I was just too tired to fight, argue, or make him go away. As soon as I opened the door one look at my flushed face and he knew something was wrong. Without any words, he hugged me and allowed me to cry on his shoulder. Even when he walked me back to the couch. He didn't say shit, not one word. He just did exactly what I needed; allowed me to be vulnerable until I fell asleep on his chest, in his arms.

And just like that, we were back. every single time I said it was the last time. We ended up in each other's arms whether emotional or sexual. This time, it was all-emotional. When I woke up the next morning, I was still in his arms. His thuggish ass had his gun poking from the small of his waist and his feet were kicked up on the table. He looked so peaceful sleeping that I didn't even want to bother him. I guess he felt me moving because he called my name. "Abbey you up?" he asked with apparent sleep in his voice. I didn't answer. I wanted to lay in his arms a little longer. When he didn't get an answer, he kissed me on the forehead and went back to sleep.

I was supposed to get up and go to work in a few hours but for now, I chose to sleep. About two hours late, Trell was shaking me to wake me up for work. I wasn't really sleeping that hard in the first place cause the back-to-back ringing of his phone disturbed my sleep long ago. I sat up yawning and rushed to go brush my teeth although I felt kind of sluggish. I really didn't want to go. I was suffering from the worst headache. When I walked out of the bathroom, Trell was sitting on the couch staring at me. "Look shorty, when you get off from work we need to talk. We need to figure out what the fuck we doin'." He told me.

"I agree." I mumbled. "In the meantime though, I have to go Trell. I'll call you."

He stood up to leave. "You wanna talk about last night and what was wrong with you?"

"Not really, at least not right now. It's been a long week." I sighed.

Trell simply stared at me and nod his head. "Aiight, if you don't wanna talk a nigga aint gone force you but I'll damn sho be back later. If you really wanna dead this shit I'll give you what you want. If you ready for some other shit then I'm with that too. Basically I'm matching whatever energy you on. Whatever you wit' I'm wit' but you gotta keep it real with me and yo'self ma." He walked over kissing me on the cheek before walking out leaving only the scent of his cologne lingering around.

Chapter 12

Leandra 'LeLe' Wells

"Hey Nicole." I spoke to the girl who was working the front register today when I walked into Jazzy's ready to work. I had planned on making a specialty dish today and just try something new. I pushed any thoughts of Cass away from my mind and made my damn mind up that this was strictly business. As long as he paid me and stayed out of the way. Nothing could take away from the fact that I'm a damn good worker and reliable as well. "Who is the new chick in the kitchen?" I asked not pleased to see somebody already back there using all of the pots and seasonings I needed.

She looked up from me and chuckled. "I assume that crazy ass Cass didn't tell you?" She shook her head. Nicole was a young girl like me; a college student just trying to make a way. She didn't work everyday though, she was only part time.

"Tell me what?"

"That's the new head cook, so you'll be sharing your hours and the kitchen with her. You're no longer in charge of the recipes; she is." Nicole shrugged. "Hell, I found out early this morning when I got here. He introduced her and then he left."

"What the fuck?" I frowned. "Cass didn't tell me anything at all. I sucked my teeth. "How does he expect me to play the back to this newbie?"

Nicole shrugged. "Shit, I don't know but that's going to be a big problem. People come up in here looking for your cooking. The new chick will be doing all the specialty menus so basically whatever she wants cooked is what ya'll gotta cook."

This shit was pissing me off. I had worked too hard and bust my damn ass to bring something special to this place only for it to be snatched away from me. I didn't know what this was about but I damn sure was going to get to the bottom of it. I stomped away to the kitchen, washed my hands, and threw on my apron, my gloves, and my hair net. "Hi, I'm LeLe." I smiled at the new head cook.

She look like she could've been in her mid 30's. She was decent looking black girl but it looked like she had a hard life. I could tell by the hard look that surrounded her. She was stirring a huge pot of whatever the hell that was she was cooking. Looking at me, she gave me a smile. "Hi, I'm Rita. You can go ahead and grab the recipe book from over there and get started on the meat for the Shepard's Pie." She told me.

I pierced my lips together to keep from saying anything. The best part of this job was having the freedom to do what I wanted. I was the one that gave out recipes and told them what to cook and now she wanted me to follow her recipe? I knew how to make a Shepard's Pie with my eyes closed; I didn't need her ingredient book to do so either. I snuck off to the side and called Cass. He didn't pick up. Only sent me a text letting me know he would be here this afternoon and to get acquainted with the new head cook. That hurt son-of-a-bitch was deliberately trying to fuck with me. The only thing I could think of was that he found out I went to see CoCo and he didn't like it. Him pulling this kind of stunt was showing me exactly how he really was. I didn't like this passive aggressive type of shit.

Instead of following Rita's recipes, I continued to do my own and I knew she wasn't pleased. I didn't give a damn. Everybody knew that the Shepard Pie specialty was only sold on Friday's and here she was serving it in the middle of the week trying to give it a totally different taste. Today was supposed to be the neck-bone soup specialty. Imagine how many customers walked out on us when they found out that's not the specialty we were serving.

Things had got so heated and so busy for Rita that she didn't know what to do. Poor girl was stressed the hell out. Halfway through the day Cass came strutting in. He stood at the door and looked at me. "LeLe, yo shift over in an hour." He looked at the A.P on his wrist.

"Excuse me?" I furrowed my brows wiping the sweat from my forehead using my handkerchief. "I close today, just like everyday."

He pointed to Rita. "She's closing. Gotta share those hours with her baby girl."

I lightly tapped my freshly manicured nails on the countertop. "Can I talk to you in private please?"

"I got a few minutes." He said looking at his watch again. "Come on." I followed him to the Office where the two big black niggas waited in front of the door. We walked inside and Cass took a seat in front of the black marble desk. He was wearing his suit look today. He grabbed some papers shifting through them. "What's up?" He asked without even looking at me.

I crossed my arms in front of my breast and looked him right in the eye. "Am I missing something? Clearly you have my number Cass. If things were going to change you could've told me."

"You should've thought about that before you went asking 21 questions about a nigga ma. You got my number, you could've called me."

"Hmm." I quizzed. "So I assume you've spoken to CoCo? Cass about that, I just needed…"

He cut me off. "It don't even matter. CoCo cant tell me shit. That's my spot. I see everything that goes on."

I swallowed a lump in my throat. "Okay, so yeah I went to see her and I ask some questions that I felt I wouldn't get the direct answer from you. Right Poochie?"

"Trust me ma, you ain't never met Poochie. You might wanna stay away from that and do yo'self a favor and stay out of my business. I'mma let you continue to work here cause I like you. However, you gotta play the back end now. I no longer trust you."

I felt like I'd been punched in the stomach. "Wait, what does that have to do with my work ethic? This is crazy. You'd let your own personal issues with me affect a working business? Wow."

"Because of the new changes, your pay getting cut to 500 a week. Rita gets the other 5. You ain't gotta close no more either."

"What?!!1" I blurted thinking about how big of a pay cut that is. I wanted to cry. All I could think about was now it was going to take me longer to save up for my restaurant. I'm so glad I didn't give Cass no pussy. That's a move I would've surely regretted. His true colors were truly coming out. I'm smart enough to know he was trying to taunt me right now. I refused to let him see me sweat though. "I get it. If I'm not fucking with you how you want, then shit changes. I gave you the power to feed me, so you have the power to starve me. I see what's going on."

He leaned back in his chair and rolled a joint. "I'mma need you to remember that." He told me with a straight face. "Now, you can take everything for what it is since you wanted to know so bad, and things can go back to how they were. We can act like none of this shit happened. I'll get her ass outta here right now. Or you can go play the back and deal with your pay cut."

I wanted to just fucking vomit. "Cass ain't no way I'll sell my soul like that. I've been through worse. I'll gladly take my pay cut. Fuck this." I walked out leaving him staring at my backside. He could kiss my entire fucking ass. Fuck what he was talking about. If he wanted to use Rita's dry ass recipes we could do allat. Fuck him.

I made my way to the back to the locker and grabbed all of my shit before walking out. "You leaving?" Nicole asked.

"Yeah, my shift got cut. I won't be closing no more."

She looked disgusted. "Cass needs his ass whooped." She whispered. "My uncles some OG's in the game. They warned me about his ass. I've been looking for a new job ever since but it's hard to find a job that pays what he does doing what I'm doing."

"Yep. It's all good though girl." I grilled. "Fuck him. I'll see you tomorrow." I told her.

The next few days went by and I mostly scanned the paper and the intranet looking for locations as well as what kind of licensing I would need to open up my own soul food spot. When I wasn't doing that I was working and staying out of Cass's fucking way. I hadn't seen much of anybody either. Seemed like now days everybody was so wrapped up in their own bullshit that nobody had time for each other. Shit was just falling apart. I still hadn't even had the chance to call Karter back and congratulate her on the baby or nothing.

Abbey had called me multiple times as well. I just simply didn't have time to call her ass back either. Right now, I had to figure out my own fucking plans. I sat Indian style in the middle of my room counting all of my money. At $4,000 a month, I was able to save a little under 25k. It would've been more but I had my car note, my insurance, my life necessities, and I'd been helping my mama with bills as well. It seemed like a lot but I still needed more. This pay cut really put a damper in my shit. Cass was trying to get in my good graces, but I wasn't budging. Type of nigga hide his own child? Even me working for him was a risk knowing what I knew.

After I counted the money and put it back in a safe place, I went to shower and take my ass to sleep since I had to work in the morning. I was opening and Rita was closing. Jazzy's only opened in the mornings twice a week. Those were my happiest days cause I didn't have to do any of Rita's breakfast specials. I still had that part on lock.

When it was time for me to open my eyes again it wasn't even because of my alarm. It was because my mama was standing over me telling me the tow was taking my truck. "Wake up LeLe. You ain't paid ya truck note? The people out there towing your shit."

"What?!" I rubbed the sleep from my eyes, grabbed my robe and flew out of the house. "Um excuse me! What the hell are you doing?"

The dude continued to attach the truck. "I have orders from the owner to come and get this truck and return it to who it belongs to." He looked at the paperwork.

"Wait, what? I'm the owner." I pulled my papers from the glove compartment.

He looked over mine and then looked over his again. "No ma'am this truck is registered to a Mr. Casanova McClein. There must be some kind of misunderstanding with the paperwork. I mean, you can go back to the dealer and find out but the truck is his."

"So who the fuck have I been paying the note to all of this time?" I quizzed. "This is some bullshit!" I realized that I had been paying the money to the company Cass gave me the information for. That doesn't mean it's a legitimate company or maybe it was just another one of his multiple connections.

"You may want to talk to Mr. McClein about that, but right now, this truck is leaving with me." He said rudely before hopping in his tow truck speeding off.

I wanted to fucking scream! I turned around feeling defeated only to see my mama at the door watching me.

She only gave me the 'I told you so' look but she didn't say it. She shook her head. "Malik would've never pulled no shit like that. These damn men be butt ass hurt now days."

I just sucked my teeth.

"You need my car for the day?" She asked me.

I nod my head 'yes' cause I knew that I would. I hated I had to spend my own money but I had to get me a car and I didn't want shit with payments since every dollar really counted right now. I'd have to suck it up and buy me something cash to get me around from point A to point B; it didn't need to be fancy. It just needed to get the job done. I called Nicole and let her know I wasn't coming in to work this morning.

"Girl." She chuckled. "Cass isn't gonna like that but I'll call Rita and get her here. I'm sure she'll appreciate the extra hours."

"Fuck Cass." I mumbled. "I'll see you on my next shift." I told her before hanging up. Almost immediately Cass started calling me. I didn't even answer for him. He had me fucked up if he even thought I was going to let him control me like that. I'd show his ass. He couldn't break me. Fuck that truck. It was fancy and all but that didn't define me. If I had to get it out the mud than so be it; but he damn sure wasn't about to break me.

Chapter 13

Majestic Jones

"I told you not to trust her muhfuckin' ass." I sat across from Poochie in the warehouse doing a drop off. He could front all he wanted but I knew he was feeling LeLe more than he said. He wasn't supposed to be liking her like that anyway. All the shit he did for her ass and she didn't even appreciate that. Now Poochie had finally got on his mission to make her life a living hell. Until she apologized to my mama and me with a genuine apology; I didn't give a fuck what happened to her.

"Nigga I ain't gotta explain myself to nobody. Not even you." Cass counted the money with a joint hanging from his mouth. The nigga was hurt. His ego was hurt. I could've told him LeLe wasn't gone give a fuck about him doing all the shit he was doing. It's only one nigga that truly had her heart; even I knew that. Had this nigga stuck to the plan he wouldn't be going through what he was going through right now tryna give her ass the chance or see the good in her.

I thought the shit was funny how he confiscated her truck. At the same time though, I knew that bitch probably had a new car the same day. Might not have been the fancy shit she just had, but I knew she went and copped something cause that's how she was. She'd been to prison. I knew she wasn't gone let this shit affect her and get the best of her. A chick like LeLe was on a mission to get her life back on track. I couldn't see her allowing Poochie to be a hold up for that. He would've done better making her fall in love with his ass, slapping the bitch up, something. I just know it wasn't supposed to be like this and since he couldn't deliver, eventually, I was gonna have to just get revenge my damn self.

"You right, you ain't gotta explain shit to me. I'm just the nigga that tried to warn you." I replied grabbing my bag to leave.

"Look." Poochie took a pull from the joint. "I got a little snitch from the inside that kinda put a bug in my ear. Niggas is getting sloppy and them folks been snooping around. Stay on ya shit and keep ya people tight."

I nod my head. On the outside I was cool, but on the inside that shit had me feeling uneasy. The last thing we needed was for the Laws to be snooping around. Up until this point shit was ran tight so I didn't understand. Just off his word alone I knew it was time for me to walk away soon and real soon. One thing about it when them folks started lingering, they weren't gone just stop. "I got'chu." I slapped him up before heading out.

I bumped into Trey's quiet ass on the way out. He gave me a head nod and kept it moving. I didn't know how to feel about that nigga. He didn't give a fuck about nobody. He was one of Poochie's most loyal soldiers at that. Always looked like he was strategizing. I knew for a fact the nigga was caked up but one look at him you wouldn't even know it. Trey wasn't no flashy ass nigga. In my opinion, Poochie needed to be a lil more like him. Because of that nigga, I stopped wearing all my jewelry and shit too. It made perfect sense. Why give the Laws something to look at?

I hopped in my whip and tried to figure out my next move. I hadn't heard from Kim in days. I called a few times and she didn't answer so since I didn't have shit else to do I decided to pull up on her and check on her. The last time I'd seen her she was in a pretty fucked up predicament. Bitch tired to make me choke her ass. For that, she didn't have to worry about me sticking my dick in her ever again. I didn't need to be caught up in the moment and fuck around and catch an accidental charge for killing her ass. If she wanted to be taken out of her misery, she could do it herself.

When I got to her door, I knocked multiple times and no answer. I placed my ear to the door to see if I could hear anything; I didn't hear shit. I hoped she was aiight wherever she was. I walked back out and checked her parking spot. Her car wasn't home either. I sat back in my car and called her again only for her to not pick up. I called Abbey next. "Yo, you heard from yo girl Kim? Nigga tryna check on her."

"No I haven't, not since we came back from Orlando. Why?" She asked sounding all uneasy. I didn't know what that was about.

"Oh aiight, well if you talk to her have her to call me."

"Will do." She told me hanging up the phone in my face. "Rude bitch." I mumbled. In my book all these hoes were crazy and losing their fucking minds.

Since I had some time to spare, I decided to go and see about my mama and drop some money off. My visits had been becoming a little more limited cause I couldn't take the pressure of her pressuring me to give her a grandchild. Every fucking time, no matter what we discussed, she always wanted to bring that shit up. Like she wanted me to build a woman and the next day make her pop a baby out her ass. It just simply didn't work like that and I preached this shit over and over. Another thing that got to me was her reckless drinking and unacceptable behavior. I got tired of hiding and throwing away bottles and shit.

Every time I found one hiding spot she would just find another. Shit was crazy. I decided to call her and let her know that I was on the way to come get her for lunch. "Ma, get dressed. I'll be there to get you in a few."

"You got some money for me?" She asked.

"Yeah." I told her.

"I'm getting ready now." She told me. "I was in the middle of getting dressed anyway. I was hoping you called."

"Oh yeah?" I asked. "Where you was going?"

Silence.

"Hellooo? Ma you there?"

"You must have forgot what today is." She told me.

I thought about it and could've slapped myself. "No, I told her. I didn't. See you soon." I hung up.

I'd been so caught up I didn't even realize today is Malik's birthday. We were taking our annual trip to the cemetery to put some flowers on his grave. She was crying before we even got there. There was already some flowers on the grave when we arrived. I pulled out the card and read it:

To the love of my life. I miss you so much.
There isn't a day that goes by and my mind isn't consumed
with thoughts of you.
I love you forever. Continue to sleep well baby. Love, LeLe.

I put the card back.

"Who is that from?" My mama asked busily dusting off his headstone.

"Nobody." I lied. "Just somebody he knew I guess."

For the next two hours or so we sat and talked about old times and memories of Malik. Even when I wanted to just forget, my mama had a way of making me relive the shit. At some point she had to let him go. If she didn't, she would never make it easy for me to forgive and move the fuck on. Being around her dealing with this situation made me angry all over again. Nigga was just tired of battling with myself.

Chapter 14

Kimberly 'Kim' Laws

I sat on the toilet in my apartment staring at the positive sign on the pregnancy test. Just the thought of having a baby made me want to vomit. Shit wasn't supposed to happen like this. I'd been training people, doing parties on the side and getting high for the past few days. I completely cut myself off from the world. I had every intention on speaking my truth to Majestic and LeLe both no matter what the consequence was. If I had to die behind it than so be it. I'd seen everything besides death anyway. However, staring at the pregnancy test changed shit drastically.

How could I tell Majestic everything and then hit him with a bomb telling him I'm pregnant knowing he would never let me live. I watched the warm tears fall on my bare thighs. I knew something was off. I'd been way to moody but when I missed my period yesterday, I knew something was wrong. My shit was never late; ever. The first thing I did was run out and get a First Response pregnancy test. I sat the test on the dresser still in the wrapper contemplating about taking it before I actually got the courage and build up enough balls to even do so.

I was having an ongoing battle with myself. Hell, I didn't want to kill my baby. I had never even been pregnant before but how was I going to raise a baby as fucked up as I am? Did I really want to bring a baby in my fucked up world? At the same time, did I want to kill a blessing for my own selfish reasons? I grabbed a cold rag and wiped my face off from dried up tears. I knew if this was going to happen, I had to disappear for a while. It hurt me to know I had to leave this place, but if I wanted to protect me and my unborn then I had to do it.

I went to my bank app to check my account. I only had $500 left after paying bills. I then went to my dresser drawer and pulled out the money I had in there, which totaled to only $200. I knew that wasn't enough money. It would get me out of here but I needed more if I was going in hiding for the next few months. I didn't have not one person I could call so I called the person that I least expected. Somebody I never thought I'd have to call. When she personally gave me her cell number I didn't imagine in a million years that I would ever actually use it but here I was.

"Hello, this is Emily Bradshaw, or Bradshaw law firm services. How can I help you?" She answered.

"Um, I know this is so awkward." I sighed squeezing the phone so tight my knuckles were turning white as sweat perspired on my forehead. "Emily, this is Kim, your sister-in-law."

"Oh." She perked up. "Hi Kim. Sorry about that. I thought you may have been a client."

"It's okay." I closed my eyes and then opened them back. Fuck it. "Emily, I just didn't know who else to call."

"Is everything okay?" She asked sounding concerned.

"Not really. I need to leave here and I need help to do so. I have no money Emily and you and Karter are the only people that can help me. I called you instead of Karter because I don't know how pissed she is with me but I need help. I need a rehab and I need a place to stay for a while. I'm not asking to live with you because that wouldn't work. I'm asking to help me get on my feet. No, I'm begging Emily. For the sake of me and my unborn child."

"Kim, you are a part of Karter, which makes you my family. I'll be glad to help you. How soon can you get to Orlando?" She asked.

"I'm coming today if you say yes. I'll pack everything right now and I'm coming."

"Sure. Come on so we can figure this out. Don't you worry about Karter. I'll talk to her. I'll be in the office most of the day but when you get here make sure to give me a ring. I'll text you my assistants number just in case you can't get me. His name is Bob." She told me.

"Thank you, thank you, thank you so much Emily." I cried gratefully. When we hung up the phone, she did as promised and sent the number to her assistant. I had to do what I had to do. After I had my baby, I would return and let them do whatever they wanted to do to me after I spoke my truth but right now, my child's life was in my hands.

I took me hours to pack up everything and stuff as much as I could in my trunk and in my backseat. The next stop was to my rent office to let them know I was breaking my lease and wouldn't be returning. Everything in that apartment, they could have or do whatever the hell they wanted to do with it. After that, I made sure I went to the gas station and gassed up so I could take the ride. It was a long silent ride. I knew I had to reach out to Abbey eventually because I didn't want anyone to come to the conclusion that my ass had gotten kidnapped and end up pulling out a false missing person's report. I'd make sure

Emily and Karter knew not to give out my destination or no information on me. I knew this was selfish, but I had to do this for the kid.

If Majestic wanted to kill me after this; I pray he was ready to be a single father and take care of this baby without my help. In another sense, maybe God saw it fit to have this happen to save me from myself and to save me from Majestic when he found out the truth. By the time I made it to Orlando the sun was setting. Just like promised, Emily was available. We met at a coffee shop where I told her everything. "Emily I'm telling you this cause if anything ever happens to me this is something that needs to be known." I wiped my tears. "First thing first. Can you appoint me to a good rehab? I have to shake my drug habit Emily. I have to do this for my baby."

Emily was so sensitive that she sat at the table crying with me. I saw in her eyes that she did want to help me though. I appreciated her for that. "I'll help you Kim. A rehab cost money. I'll pay for that. It's going to help you."

"I swear I'll pay you back Emily."

She waved me off. "Don't even worry about it. You just focus on getting better and I'll take care of the rest." She assured me.

I nod my head and picked over the chocolate donut sitting in front of me. Taking a sip of my tea I stared out of the window while Emily went to cover our tab. It sucked that this is how it had to happen for me to finally want to get some help, but it was long overdue. I couldn't continue to live my life like this. See, this was the problem with people like me. We held in all the pain and hurt thinking that we could just fix ourselves. Either that or smoke and drink the problem away. In my case, snorting coke had become my best friend. In return, my own demons caused me to hurt other people who I genuinely did love. Shit wasn't fair to be hurting people who actually were in my corner when my own mama wasn't.

Thinking of her made me want to gag. I would never be the kind of mother she was. How you birth a child and choose a man over that child? That shit will mentally fuck anybody up. When she came back from paying the tab she had some good news for me. She called in a favor from a buddy from hers and I could go to the rehab first thing in the morning. "I don't want to stay at your place and I don't want to speak to Karter until you've spoken with her Emily. I'll get a room for tonight and then first thing in the morning I'll be ready for rehab."

"Sure thing." Emily gave me a warm hearted smile. She followed me to the hotel and helped me get my things inside after paying for my room and getting me settled in. When she left, I took a shower and laid across the bed. Next, I called Sprint to have my number changed. The only person I sent a text with the new number was Emily so she would be able to reach me in the morning. I was determined to start a new life and get my shit together. After all, I didn't know how much of this life left that I had to live after all of my bullshit.

Chapter 15

Leandra 'LeLe' Wells

I parked my Nissan Altima in my usual parking spot in front of Jazzy's and tried to use my key to open the door since I was opening. I had to take off for two whole days in order to get my car situation in order but it was worth it. I had found a lady on Craigslist selling a 2015 for 7k so I took it with no problem. I had to take Trell with me to make sure the car ran decent and he also paid for a Car fax report on it to make sure it hadn't had any front-end damage before, or flood damage. Once everything checked out that was it. I purchased me a new tag and added my insurance. The car was a big downgrade from my truck and Lord knows I missed it already but nobody was going to just punk me like that.

I wiggled my keys in the lock only to discover it wasn't working at all. What the hell? I pound on the door hoping that Nicole was in there and she was. She came to the door and unlocked it giving me a crazy look. "What the hell going on with the locks?" I asked her.

"Girl I don't know what you did to piss Cass off but he had the locks changed and told everybody to make sure they don't let you in." She shook her head. "Some real hoe shit. I know damn well I gotta hurry up and find me another job cause ion wanna be going through no shit like this with him in the future."

"Sssss." I frowned with a pure look of disgust. "He's such a bitch ass nigga! He wants me to run behind him and beg and I'm not gonna do it. Fuck him." I cried.

Nicole stepped out and consoled me. "You'll find something else LeLe and whether he knows it or not, he needs you more than you need him. Maybe you should try to just have an adult conversation with him."

"I tried that."

"Try again, men are just hard to get through at times. You know them niggas childish girl. We mature way faster."

I thought about what she said. Maybe it was in my best interest to just clear the air with him. I wanted to continue to work here cause I needed the money but I wanted nothing more than a business relationship with him; at least until I could get my own restaurant. That bracelet her purchased for me, I even planned on giving the shit back but since he wanted to play like this, I'd pawn it knowing I could get a nice chunk of change. See, Cass was used to women playing by his rules but I wasn't CoCo. He could deal with his child's mother in that way but not me. I wasn't having it.

"Yeah, you're right." I told her.

After I left, went home first to change out of my work clothes and then drove straight to Cass's house knowing he was there. I decided to park down the street and on the side of the road and take the walk to his house. I didn't even want my shit parked in front of his house to give him the pleasure of trying to clown me. If he didn't want to hear me out that was cool, but at least he could pay me the damn money he owed me for the week. His car was in the driveway along with a few others and Trey as well. I hopped out and knocked hard on the door.

I was met with Trey standing there looking at me crazy. "What you doing here shorty?" He looked like he wasn't pleased to see me. "Cass know you here? You shouldn't be here right now." He frowned. "Leave man, and don't come back."

I peeked over his shoulder and saw straight out to the back where the pool was. There was Cass along with some other niggas including Majestic. Looked like they were having some kind of meeting. "Look I come in peace aiight? I just need to speak with Cass. It'll be real quick." He simply shook his head and moved out the way. "You women are so fuckin' hard headed man I swear. Aiight go ahead."

"Thank you." I replied with attitude.

I went straight to the back and through the sliding door. "Cass, can I talk to you for a minute?" I didn't know what they were talking about but it looked deep. When they saw me they all stopped talking and stared making me feel uncomfortable.

"Wussup baby girl?" Cass looked up asking me.

I wanted to fucking spit in his face. "In private." I said. I knew he could see the steam bouncing off of me.

"Go inside, I'll meet you in there in a minute. We wrapping it up now." He told me.

I sucked my teeth and made my way inside to sit down. Trey grilled me the entire time. I patiently waited until he adjourned his little meeting. When he sent them all in a different direction to get whatever the hell it was they needed out of his house. "Clear it out." He told them.

"We'll be up north for two weeks." He told them and then stared at me. "So what's on your mind pretty girl?" He asked once again taunting me. "Come to your senses yet?"

Now it was my turn to make his ass wait. "Can I use the restroom before we get into this?" I asked.

"Shit, you know where it's at. I'll be here." He let me walk off to the restroom.

When I closed the door and locked it, I put my face over the sink throwing some water on my face before looking at myself real good. I wasn't no weak ass bitch and Cass had me fucked up to the max. I literally had to get myself together to stop from exploding. At the same time, I was losing it because I didn't know what my next move would be. How stupid of me to trust my life in his hands. It took me a minute to get myself together, but right before I got ready to walk out there was a big ass commotion. "Get on the ground! Get on the ground!" Was all I heard.

I swung the door open with my heart beating fast as fuck. "What the hell?" I mumbled. From the upstairs hallway I could see Cass being laid out on the ground. My heart dropped to my ass when I saw the FEDS up in this bitch. I was stuck. Wasn't no way I was going down with these niggas. I prepared to take off. I rather had taken my chances running rather then walk into that bullshit there. This shit didn't look right. I'm a convicted felon on probation and at this niggas house. This was a terrible case of wrong place at the wrong time.

Before I could even get my feet to move a hand was being wrapped around my mouth from the behind. immediately the tears fell from my eyes out of fear. My breathing got heavy as fuck. "If you wanna make it outta here… shut the fuck up." He growled in my ear. I couldn't make out the voice, all I knew was my life was flashing right before my eyes. The colors of those prison cells appeared so vividly in my mind. It wasn't supposed to go down like this… nah… not like this!

To be continued.....

CPSIA information can be obtained
at www.ICGtesting.com
Printed in the USA
LVHW081745280220
648532LV00010B/725